D0742424

AN UNNAMED PRESS BOOK

Published in North America by the Unnamed Press.

www.unnamedpress.com

Hardcover ISBN: 9781951213541
eISBN: 9781951213558

Library of Congress catalog data available upon request.

An earlier version of the story "A Fresh Start," formerly called "A Fresh Start Ruined," first appeared in *McSweeney's Quarterly Concern* (2020); as well as the story "Brother," formerly called "Lawton," which first appeared in *Yellow Medicine Review* (2018).

Designed and typeset by Jaya Nicely

Manufactured in the United States of America by McNaughton & Gunn

Distributed by Publishers Group West

First Edition

A CALM & NORMAL HEART

CHELSEA T. HICKS

stories

The Unnamed Press
Los Angeles, CA

na^tse wacpe wida, howaiki shche?
dada^ ozhu hlok'a thikaxa pe
tsexope a^oxda cka katho^ tsexope eko^ mi^kshe
howaiki shki bre tsi wida paxe na^
ithape ena^ kako^ dada^ zani doda hu da apa
kako^da wathusho^da^
a^zhi na^tse wacpe
howaiki etsi dxa^ atsi hi^e?

my functional heart, where are you?
what turned you into an empty glass
is it that I love the spiders & am like one
wherever I go making my house
I have only to wait & all things come to me
& therein break their necks
but a calm & normal heart
where does that come from?

TABLE OF CONTENTS

AUTHOR'S NOTE

Wazhazhe people are currently revitalizing our language, which is called Wazhazhe ie. Due to limited recognition of Indigenous characters in fonts, I use Latinized spellings rather than the Wazhazhe ie orthography created by Herman "Mogri" Lookout. This orthography, depicted on the cover of the book as well as in chapter titles, is the written language of Wazhazhe ie, which translates literally as "Osage talk." As Wazhazhe elder Myron Red Eagle once told me, spellings in our language may vary from person to person. I have reflected that quality of the living language in my usages within these stories. I hope my inclusion of the language will support Wazhazhe ie, and the practice of including Indigenous languages broadly in literature.

—Chelsea T. Hicks

A CALM & NORMAL HEART

TSEXOPE
𐓍𐓘𐓷𐓪𐓰𐓘

One time between a breakup and a shackup, I went home for a visit. I had most of my stuff in my car but I didn't really want to move into my aunt's place, so I went to the laundrymat to procrastinate. I parked right across the street from the yellow house where my iko used to live all the times she divorced my grandfather. An old man was traveling down the street, headed west via lawn mower, and an orange tabby cat greeted me as I roamed in and started up the laundry. There was no one else around. I sat in the gentle breeze from the open windows and listened to the grasshoppers sing on the long grass of the hill behind the building as I opened an old newspaper. Inside was an article dated from two summers ago, telling about *the movie*.

The movie went without introduction among Wazhazhe people, as it was telling one of our stories at the hand of a big-name director with a cast of equally famous celebrities. They were filming the story of how I^shdaxi^ spouses of my ancestors had murdered them with the plan of inheriting our oil money. This had happened to many of our ancestors, and the film was sending a shock wave through the tribe, as we did not often talk openly about old traumas. At the end of the article, there was a call for actors, with audition information. Like most Wazhazhe people living in town, I'd auditioned, but I was not one of the few who made it.

As I folded the paper up, an older woman emerged from the laundrymat's office. She was I^shdaxi^, in cargo shorts.

She addressed me. "Are you with the film?"

"Hello. No," I said. "Are you? I thought the film had wrapped."

She shrugged. "I heard something was happening tonight. At the museum." As she spoke, she eyed my blue Mustang parked outside. She didn't bother to answer my question, but she kept standing there, so I told her whose relative I was. She didn't seem to know the names but waddled off like an old turtle anyhow, satisfied with this barest of info. I changed my laundry over, thinking of her I^shdaxi^ ancestors and the courthouse they'd built to try themselves for their own murders, never referring to our ancestors as people but always only as *the Indian.* I thought about going up there to roll a cigarette and stare at the downtown.

My phone buzzed.

> Are you going to the museum thing? Buh you didn't tell me you were home.

I'd been in town all of thirty minutes and my whereabouts were known and circulating. The laundrymat woman had probably gotten on Facebook and started spreading gossip out of boredom. Or not. I mean, what was there to report? *Woman with stuff in her car arrives in town*? There was nothing they could do but speculate, as I had kept to myself and pretty much stayed out of trouble. I went outside to the curb and sat while I rolled a cigarette from tobacco and other plants I kept in my pocket. The cool wind was nice, not strong enough to challenge my rolling.

An old friend passed by in a teal Nissan but didn't see me. It was the turn of the hour, nearing dusk. Cars crisscrossed intersections in a scramble. Up the hill, the courthouse towered over it all like a throne blocking the sun. I stared at it, imagining my great-grandmother's trial, how each one of her witnesses mysteriously disappeared and never returned.

It was my opinion that ghosts lounged alongside the resident owls in the eaves of the building. The tobacco made me feel like I could bear to go up there and try to talk to her spirit, but I had been so tired, almost too tired to move. I was strangely comforted by my laundry tumbling in thumps behind my back.

More texts came in on my phone—something really was going on at the museum—and people wanted me to respond or commit to meeting up. I watched as cars headed up the hill, past the courthouse. It was the first tribal museum in the country, and we were proud of it. Maybe I could manage seeing all those people in their foldout chairs on the lawn for whatever was happening. Last time I'd gone up there, I'd seen some moccasins sculpted in clay. I wanted to have the pleasure of seeing them again. I got up and just started walking, leaving my laundry behind as I headed toward Grandview. With each step, the courthouse loomed. Made of copper turned green, with Corinthian columns, it was a symbol of the assimilation forced and facilitated by our oil wealth, the United States government, and the boarding school little more than a stone's throw away. My iko had attended that school and slept handcuffed to her bed by the nuns so she couldn't run away. That was the reason I barely spoke my language and now studied it.

Through the interconnected parking lots, I took the least visible route, behind the chief's office toward the museum's long lawn. I saw a screen set up, as large as a movie theater's, and beyond the white square of fabric, a crowd of Wazhazhe people in powwow chairs. This wasn't an art thing, but a movie, a sort of drive-in without cars. I saw one of the friends who'd been texting. Under his flat-brim, he had severe bone structure and a slim figure. He watched me.

I went over to him, with his black jean jacket and his hat reading PROTECTOR. He was Normcore Native Cool. Just the sight of him almost made me laugh, thinking of the old pickup line *I couldn't help but notice you noticing me…*

"Hawe," he said. "Tha^tsie."

"Hawe da^he. Atsipe." I motioned around to everyone there.

"Da^he. Ma^ze ie owado^e ada^ka kaxe." He nodded at the big screen.

"Hi^tse thuza ma^thi^. Do^pa dada^ othatse thaishe?"

"Dada^ a^thatse da^kadxai?"

"Are you asking me to dinner?" I said. We smiled at my mistake of switching to English, and our ability to understand each other.

"So are you in the film or what?" he said.

"No," I said. "Everyone keeps asking."

"They're wondering why you're here."

"Oh," I said, like I didn't already know. I never knew what to say to him.

"So what brings you back this time?"

"A job." To myself, I added that I was simply *in need of one*. Plus, shelter. I also reminded myself it was all right to be private about my own business. I just didn't like people knowing things about me. A black wolf spider crawled onto my moccasin. We both noticed it and intuited the message: I was on my own, and strong enough to be living my life that way.

He motioned for me to sit beside him.

"Ha^ko washchila tha^she?" he said.

I sat. "What am I thinking about?" I wasn't sure I understood.

"Howe." He nodded yes.

The things I thought most about were my dreams, which were of walking in dried creek beds of carved red clay called the Paths of Sorrow. I had repeating dreams of walking red earth with school children toward wooden staircases like the ones used as queues for old coasters.

"Ipaho^ ma^zhi." *I don't know.*

He searched my face, wanting to know more, I guess, but I didn't look back at him. My old best friend walked by. I almost said her last name. Cygne, which means *swan*. She'd become a devout Christian and I wasn't in the mood to be evangelized. She wore her hair gelled in crispy black curls, or strands processed straight, depending on the day and her mood. Curly today, which contrasted with her eyes sunk in liner and her hands clutching a book.

I stood. "I got laundry going down there," I said, and indicated the bottom of the hill.

"Want company?" my friend asked from under his flat-brim.

"You'll miss the movie."

"Yeah, but I've missed you."

"Wow." I laughed. "Eshe." I had not been expecting that. I felt myself getting nervous as we went down the hill and made our way to the laundrymat. My mind stayed blank, and I focused on minute details to stay calm, twigs and leaves crushed into the corners of the concrete steps, and the tattoo on his forearm. I wondered if the woman would put out more gossip, or if this visiting was hugely uneventful, and I was being absurd from too much time spent alone. The laundrymat let off steam through vents, and I anticipated the clothes warming the tips of our fingers.

"I worry about you," he said.

"Why?" I said.

He nodded toward my car and held the door for me. "Doesn't seem like you'll ever come back. All that stuff in your car."

I didn't know what to say, so I kept to my silence.

He took his phone out and showed me a picture of a piece of paper. "This is what we're doing out here," he said. "See what you think."

Thi^kshe Kshe Dxa^ Tse The Ke Pa The She Ka E The apa/apai

I imagined myself **Thi^kshe** SITTING / ROUND SINGULAR ANIMATE OR INANIMATE in the middle of my rug back in the home of my ina in Kawazhi Dawa^ I imagined myself **Kshe** LYING / LONG SINGULAR ANIMATE OR INANIMATE ENTITY on my bed in a hoodie, alone for once, headphones in. I imagined myself **Dxa^** STANDING SINGULAR ANIMATE ENTITY in a clean room, wherever it was, drinking a smoothie after vacuuming. I imagined myself **Tse** STANDING SINGULAR INANIMATE ENTITY because I had stood there so long I had become a lamp, a dead tree, a bolt of metal I became in my imagining **The** MOVING SINGULAR ANIMATE ENTITY and I left my room, or my apartment, or my house, and went to Bartlesville Wal-Mart, where there were **Ke** SCATTERED PLURAL INANIMATE ENTITIES many, many plastic objects being ogled purchased possessed by **Pa** PLURAL ANIMATE ENTITIES, which created incredible yearly waste hoarding in **The** THIS where **She** THAT was making **Ka** THESE, THIS, THIS ONE into **E** THAT ONE, THAT PERSON, SHE/HER, HE/HIM, THOSE PERSONS, THIS (PRAGMATICALLY OBVIOUS) PERSON OR THINGS, THE FOREGOING, SHE HERSELF, HE HIMSELF, THEY THEMSELVES all those who were buying littering dying and in this imagining I questioned, “And why could I not be **The apa/apai** OVER THERE APART and yet become **Nika Thali^** A GOOD MAN” and to myself I replied, “Well, I am interdependent here and she who I see as **Wak’o^ Thali^ Wida** A GOOD WOMAN WHO IS MINE is not at that location at this time.”

"What is this?" I finally said, after I'd read the whole thing. Judging by the last line, I thought maybe he was flirting. He had finished folding my laundry. It was all done. I began to apologize, but he shrugged, and I laughed. "I love it," I said, handing him back his phone.

"Yeah," he said, showing his dimples. Our hands touched when I returned his phone.

I stood. "Want to go to Tulsa?" I said. I didn't know what I was saying, but the idea seized me and I seized it back. "Real quick," I added, absurdly. "We could go to The Colony and listen to a show. There's a Cherokee-language band playing there tonight, I think."

He stood, immediately ready, and I quickly turned away to hide the smile on my face. We went outside and while I made space in my car, I thought of my life back in Los Angeles. I imagined dancing at La Cita, where the Indigenous motherfuckers there, as an ex had called them, didn't differentiate between Mexican and Native, and we didn't have to divide ourselves like cold slices of butter the way we did here. I felt the need to enact some type of violence. I started the engine.

"About what you wrote," I began, not knowing what exactly I was going to say. "There's so many people in the world, and we all speak English. I don't want to be limited to the people here, or to our tribe. I don't think people have to be with someone in the tribe, or even with another Native, for that reason. If that's what you meant by showing me the poem thing."

"Controversial," he said. "Some women are good at getting men."

"What?" I was confused. "What is that supposed to mean?"

"I mean, maybe you're just saying that to be a tease. Or you're saying it because you *do* want to be with someone in the tribe, and I'm your only viable option, and you're baiting me."

I laughed. How had we gotten here? This was the longest conversation we'd ever had. His out-loud analysis was good, but he hadn't pegged me. I wondered if I regretted this outing.

"Maybe we ought to go back to that film," I said.

"I'm in it," he said.

"Oh, wow. Well, I'm sorry I didn't ask. Maybe we should go back, if you want to."

"No," he said, and I could hear joy in his voice. I wished I could see him. From the way his voice traveled, I could tell he was looking at me, but my seat was farther forward than his so I couldn't even catch him in my peripherals. He was tall, probably as tall as I would be if I were a man. I focused on taking the curves in the road smoothly.

"Do you roll cigarettes?" I asked. "There's some tobacco in the glove box."

He laughed. "You smoke? Na^niopazhi. Cowboy killers." But he opened it and he rolled. "You could get some man out there in L.A.," he continued, picking back up on the topic I now wanted to avoid. I had spoken bluntly like that to intimidate him, but he was more comfortable than I was, and he had easily called my bluff. He was still going, getting bolder with each word.

"*Not* that there are any Wazhazhe men for you. But our men, aren't they the ones that need you? And more generally, every man wants to be needed. However, a woman that needs her man too much will become unhappy. It's peo a^katha, when a woman sees that a man knows how to do something and she does, too. You have that."

"Philosopher?" I said, not exactly following him, but meaning to tease anyway. He handed me the cigarette and lit it. It was nice having his hand near my mouth, and I put on Tears for Fears in my CD player and thought of my life in SF, where the DJs and the drag queen cover bands had everyone dancing through the club like tumbleweeds. My date and I touching each other's backs as we danced, and me never knowing if there would be a bottle of whiskey or a gun or nothing tucked into the back of their jeans under the hem of a silky shirt.

"So you're a city girl," he said when the song ended. "You like Tulsa, huh?"

"Well. You want to ride around drinking in a truck on the back roads? Or what?"

He shrugged. "You don't have to drink."

"I get really bored when I don't drink," I said.

"You could bead. Watch some TV. But... Diet Coke and whiskey it is," he said. I let him choose his own music next, and we listened to the Rolling Stones. I skipped "Under My Thumb" but otherwise let the whole album play until we got downtown. There was no show at The Colony, so we went to Mercury Lounge. We listened to Americana under a blue neon sign.

BIG

BAD

LUV

"I guess this is boring, too," I said after a couple of songs.

He laughed. "Everyone here is ugly," he said.

"You're ugly," I said.

"Am not."

We laughed. I tried to play footsie with him but my foot got caught on the metal post under the table, and I accidentally kicked him. We play-kicked each other under the table. Hooking up with him was starting to seem like a good idea.

"I want to take you to this place called Movot Point," I told him. "But it has a *V* missing."

"So...Moot Point?" he said.

"Exactly."

He kissed me then, and I kissed him back. I didn't know what was happening, but that was how it began, and I'd had about as much serious conversation from him as I could take.

He pulled away. "Let's go now?" he said.

"You want to bead and watch TV."

"Yeah…or something."

"Fine," I said. "But one more song."

A FRESH START

ᏍᏁ ᏏᏌᏍᏦᏁ

1956

The Monday after Florence married her boss, she went into his office and told him dinner would be ready at six.

"Sales reports?" he asked.

She hesitated, skirt swishing nylons. "Done."

"One more thing." Jim hung a cigarette from his lips and tapped the corner of his mouth.

Florence kissed him the way he liked, lips extra soft, no spit, then slid the keys off his desk. He said nothing, so she bit the smile from her cheeks and walked out of the office. No one ever drove Jim's Pontiac, but here she was, stepping into the parking lot at 4:30 in the afternoon, tracing the creamy paint job, her new diamond ring reflecting sun off the hip bone curves of the hood. Her eldest son and his wife would be envious when they saw the car tonight. Meeting a new daughter-in-law on their own first night home as newlyweds was not ideal, but nothing about her life was ideal, except for Jim. She rolled the windows down like she didn't care and drove home to check on David John, her six-year-old.

He was supposed to come home straight after school, no more roaming the neighborhood, what with dirt-caked elbows and baseball bruises. This was Jim's new rule, delivered the same easy way he'd said he'd lie, tell the county clerk he was Cherokee if they so much as eyed her. At Johnstone Avenue, she braked for the light and a teen boy clacked up behind her. He walked by, swinging his hips in gabardine and dress shoes, pounding the sidewalk. His gait reminded her of her first son's father. The light went green and her thoughts moved away from her and seemed to occur on the windshield as the boy continued on his way down the street. An ache grew between her shoulder blades, the place echo always said her ancestors touched, supporting her. Her foot hesitated over the gas pedal. She checked that no one was behind her and put the car into park. Then she changed lamé pumps for loafers, took three aspirin, and hit the gas, speeding away from the sense of unreality that was meant to remain on the before side of the marriage.

A white owl flew from a tall cedar and floated low over the lawns where sprinklers stuttered into tiny rainbows. She reached her one-story limestone house, where the bike-free yard confirmed her latchkey kid was out, and went directly next door to ask the redhead nurse if she'd seen him. The door opened on the fifth knock, and the neighbor shook her head no, David John wasn't in the living room trading stories for pie. No one else even opened their door. All down the block, women hid behind peepholes, mixed-bloods hating her the same as the whites they resembled, each identifying her as Indian divorcée.

She turned onto Osage Avenue and went down that block, knocking with diligence, but still no one opened. Maybe this was punishment for her transformation from Mrs. Groves into Mrs. Haydon in the span of a year. She faced the yellow-blue sun-fade and went home to call her ex-husband, Frank.

His new wife answered and said they hadn't seen David John since July fourth.

Florence thanked the severe lisp of a woman and hung up.

At her son's age, she'd had a dead mother, a disappeared father, and an aunt who hit her daily, but she hadn't run away. Growing angry, she went back outside and bellowed his name from the porch.

Wind blew the flush off her skin. Jim would be home any minute to reduce her to Future Mother, Incapable. He wanted a son of his own, badly, and she could see him rationing affection like ice into dinner party glasses, a kiss here, a hand squeeze there. On the third date, he'd said he wanted to make so much money he could pay for a full tomb, like Jesus's. Jim also said his mother's love was like a mink stole, but Florence knew her love would be even better. She felt love like water: it went everywhere—dispersed, evaporated, gathered overhead until it flooded everything. Six dates in, she'd still declined to go home with him, because rejection made her more than secretary-flavored candy.

"Someone needs to oversee all this." That's what he told her when he proposed.

It was true that she was full of peo a^katha, as her grandmother called it. Know-how. In loving, keeping house, rearing children. Still, she'd have to work harder to make up for being on her second time around, and a missing son on day one? She feared that could start the fight that would begin the end of the marriage, before it had properly begun.

She descended the steps, walked the driveway, and slammed herself into the car seat, the cement whirling about her in a bout of vertigo. Clouds piled above the rooftops and a train screeched in the distance. She buckled, revved, and reversed toward a man in her rearview mirror. His car was parked in front of her yard, and he was rummaging inside for something.

She got out to ask if he'd seen her son, but just then the telephone rang in the house and she ran back inside, leaving the engine running in the driveway.

It was her ex-husband.

"I haven't called the police yet. Have you seen him, Frank? Is he there?"

There was silence for a moment, then: "No. Where is he, Florence? He's your only goddamn responsibility."

Florence pictured the striped overalls she'd sewn for the baby that had turned out to be a second daughter, Vera—whom Frank had wanted to be a boy. It was usually Vera's job to find David John, but piano practice had spared her today. The receiver crackled with a pop and thud, the dropping of a heavy tool. Florence made a fist and matched it to a pink rose on her wallpaper.

"I married Jim."

"Florence, what in hell happened?"

"I took him to the Arkansas office, where they don't ask for a birth certificate."

"I mean, where's David John? What happened to our son?"

"You don't have to always treat me like a wad of crap."

"Call if he doesn't come back tonight."

Florence nodded to the silence that replaced Frank's voice. She'd spent years plying his miser's smile with pie and chicken-fried steak, but gave up the moment Vera grabbed onto his dinner chair at three years old and he shoved her, nearly knocking her over. He'd tried blaming the chicken, saying, "It's too goddamn salty!" All angry Neolithic brow, mangled left ear, one-quarter Cherokee, three-quarters Irish, with a full frown deepening into early wrinkles. In reply, Florence had ripped off the locket containing his photo and dropped it into his gravy pool. Then she'd collected Vera and left the house.

Now she pulled the phone to the floor, dialed the police, and filed a report.

Then she called her half brother, Billy.

He picked up on the first ring. "Florence?"

"It's me." Her brother's voice was like a valve releasing her.

"I just knew. I could feel you were gonna call."

She laughed and then sobbed, sputtering out that David John was missing, the neighborhood women wouldn't help find him, Frank had insulted her, and now she was married to Jim, who didn't know David John was gone and would not understand, and on top of it all Roy was coming with his new wife for dinner and she wasn't ready.

"I'll be damned!" Billy was the only person she'd told everything to, down to the very end, when Frank had insulted the smallness of her eyes, the freckle on her right foot, her hairless arms, the bridge of her nose, the shape of her breasts. "Well, how long's the kid been gone?"

"Hours!" Florence's stomach shuddered like a twitchy eye.

"He'll come back. Now, ask me how my cattle been—get your mind off things."

Florence pulled the phone cord tight along her leg. "How are they, Billy?"

"They've been asking the same thing about you."

Florence's laugh bounced in the receiver.

"I ran away at DJ's age. Wrapped cheese in a bandanna on a stick. If he's not back in another hour, call me."

"Okay. Love you."

"You too, kid."

They hung up and the living room filled with the ticking of clocks. Her son's head could be split open on the concrete, bike slid down into a gully. He might have tried to dodge a car and ended up smashed between a lamppost and a fender. The old sadness crawled up her shoulder blades, around her neck, and lodged itself in her mouth. It was the same feeling as ever: romantic in fall, hard in winter; worst in spring, except when she was in love; fullest in summer, when it wore her like a thick coat, crushing with heavy time. If she pushed all her attention into some object, the sadness would gather in her hand so she could wear it compact like a pretty brooch. A spiderweb shook on the sill. Florence gazed hard like she would become silk. She was still covered in a grief that laminated her from happiness and made her untouchable as a field of butterfly wings. Spiders could drop from the roof and carry her away and she would believe it was as unreal as everything else. That was better than crying until her eyelids were swollen and she had nightmares of child demons with round faces and slick skin.

A knock sliced the air and she jumped, hand-over-heart rattled.

She ran to the front door and yanked it open to her son, his small pink pig-runt hand in the hand of a tall bald policeman. She sank and hugged him with a low moan, but he was wet. Black asphalt imprinted them both like a fresh coat of spray paint. The bodice of her dress was ruined and now she would have to take it apart and resew the top. There was no time for that.

The policeman offered her a handkerchief. “Mrs. Groves?”

David John grabbed her hand. “Her name isn’t Groves! It’s Haydon.”

“Mrs. Haydon, then.”

Florence stood. “David John, please.” She accepted the hankie. “Thank you.”

The policeman had caught sight of the Cassatt copy over the mantel, a painting of a mother feeding her baby, one breast uncovered. His gaze went to Florence’s stained chest and he flushed. “Your boy here was out on Hillcrest, covered in fresh-laid road. Bike wreck. His sister cleaned him up. Her boyfriend banged his bike wheels back circular, too.”

“Boyfriend?” Neither of her girls had a boyfriend. Was Lora sipping tea off Hillcrest, a letter jacket pulled over her lemon-yellow sweater?

David John was still as a sentry, hands in fists.

Florence pulled him inside and thanked the officer again.

“Sure thing.” He winked. “Runaways is regular. Don’t take it too hard.”

Florence nodded, said good night, and shut the door.

David John plopped onto the couch and shoved his hands between his legs.

The skin of his left arm was shades lighter than his right. Last night's bath had been so much splashing and this, the arm, was all that had been washed.

She gripped him. "You little liar."

His mouth drifted open.

"You know what Jim says about mouth breathing!"

He closed his mouth with a look of hatred that pulled on her as if they were magnetized.

"Tell me," she said. "I feed you, clothe you, get you little presents, make sure you're taken care of, that you go to school, bathe, but do I get any thought from you?" She was unfurling out of the cocoon of her body, sending out heartbeats, but he just sat there squeezing his dirty forearm and then watching the handprint fade. "Look at me!"

He showed her eyes hard as metal and flattened his lips.

"You will respect me, and that is the first thing you will always do."

His eyes fell away from her.

"Do you know what it is to be Osage? It means to show respect."

"Great-Grandma said it means 'Name Giver' or 'Water People' or 'Perfect.'"

"Don't interrupt me." She walked to the mantel, where a portrait of David John in a suit sat beside a daguerreotype of her grandfather wearing a severe look after a council meeting. "Being Osage means things need to be done correctly. You didn't want to wear that suit, but that's what respect is." She tapped the frame of her son's picture for emphasis, but it fell and bounced onto the carpet.

"To step in the arbor, one's ribbon, beads, yarn, and pleats must fall just so. Perfect, or not at all. So with this house, so with you, so with our life. You will not run away again, ever, so long as you live. Roy's married and long gone, and Lora's one foot out the door. You think you're going to be all gone now, too?" Florence stood tall with her words. "Don't shame me. Not in front of the whole neighborhood, just as we begin a new life. Now go to your room."

He obeyed, slump-shouldered and disorderly as a puppy.

She was doing her best by him, correcting where needed. For Lora, it might be too late. She was on track to go repeating after her mother. Infatuation, baby, dropout, move, marriage, divorce. No, Lora could not have a boyfriend. Florence would set the table and then give her son a further talking-to about lies. But when she took a step she heard the crunch of the picture frame. Glass shards entered her arch and she bled her son's image into a headless blot. The pain came last, like a thin needle, just as Vera entered with piano books under arm, pink sweater fluffy as cotton candy and draped in angles over her hips. Something about Vera's thinness was wrong for this dingy neighborhood of lightly chipping paint jobs and chain-link fences.

Florence picked the glass from her foot while Vera watched her in silent judgment.

Pressure moved behind Florence's eyes. Her vision edged in gray. "I need you to fry up some chicken."

Florence never let Vera cook, but Vera nodded like this was normal.

"Fried chicken is page one hundred ten in the Lookout cookbook. Boil potatoes, beans."

Vera left the room in a silent glide. Florence had always liked this way of not speaking. Her too-perfect second daughter, who hadn't uttered a word until she was four years old. There had been self-possession in it, breaking into fully developed speech at the last possible moment. David John would never be as composed as she or as fearless as Lora, but he would learn respect. Two men to leave her, one mother to die, and she asked for one thing: a son to love her. She ran her fingers along her leather belt, beaded in a beautiful chevron pattern of red, yellow, and blue with accents of white and black, and then slid it from her waistband.

He was face down in the center of the bed when she walked in. She whipped him twice, hoping it would be enough, but he did not make any sound or movement. She lifted the belt again and continued to whip him. It was necessary that he cry, to show remorse, or else it just hardened the child. He wriggled as she lifted the belt for a final strike, and the master thread holding the beads broke in midair. Beads of red, white, yellow, black, and blue scattered across the floor. They caught in the blue folds of the quilt. She hesitated, the belt flopping back in the air, and then she lowered it with a final snap. David John began to cry and she released her breath. If only he had felt repentant sooner. Beads rolled into the baseboards and lined the windowsills. She dropped the belt as Vera opened the door.

The waft and sizzle of frying trailed in as Vera spoke. "I did the chicken and boiled the vittles like it says. Can I go practice French at Ada's house?" She did not acknowledge the belt.

"You're already finished?" said Florence.

Vera said nothing. The bow on her braid was undone. Florence retied it, feeling her daughter's unspoken words: that she had been in there for a while. She didn't know how long.

"Fine. But be back for dinner. Roy's coming."

Vera closed the door and Florence sat on the edge of the bed and hugged David John.

He hugged her back weakly, not like her eldest son, who was clingy as lint but strong. Roy and Julie would arrive soon. She had to wrap this up, immediately.

"You have your echo's hair," she said, and rocked him like the other mothers did, correcting bad little boys and girls. "You're a little Indian boy. You be proud."

She heard her Cadillac enter the driveway. Her foot was still bloody and she needed to change her dress. David John hugged her tighter and rubbed his sweaty head on her stomach.

"Go and wash your face for dinner." She pulled away from him and stood. Her dress was still covered in tar.

"Mom. Roy is coming tonight, right? With Julie, too?"

"Yes," she said, and then shut the door to his room.

Jim was on the entry mat, untying his shoes. "Why was my car still running? And did I say you could drive it?"

"Oh." She got a sweater from the closet and buttoned it up before Jim stood. "I've been preparing for Roy and Julie. I'm so nervous."

Jim held her at arm's length and squeezed her arms three times, a code she didn't know.

"I'll make it the last time," she said, and tried to kiss him, but he held her back.

"Why are you crying?"

"I'm not," she said.

David John thudded in, still tear-streaked, but now in boots and holding a rubber lasso.

Jim released Florence and squatted to David John's height. "Hey, you."

David John approached Jim with poise. "Hi. Want to see my drawings?"

Smoke singed Florence's nose. "Do you smell that?"

David John rolled his eyes. "Been smelling it forever." He dropped the rope and ran.

In the kitchen, Florence found the burner still on, the range hot, and all the thighs charred.

Headlights entered the kitchen through the sink window.

"Roy and Julie! Already." Jim cracked the window and aired the kitchen out.

Florence ran to hide his shoes. This was her first time meeting her son's wife, and she wasn't prepared. She squared her shoulders and tried to make her face seem relaxed. It was easier, following Jim in his lazy walk, three-piece suit still creased at the knees. He gave her a quick kiss by the door. "Why don't you teach Roy's new wife how to fry pork?"

"Good idea." She kissed the stripe of white hair sprouting from his temple and they stepped out to catch Roy in the driveway, holding a casserole dish with one arm and his wife with the other.

The wife turned. Her purple skirt opened like an evening primrose. "Mr. and Mrs. Haydon!" She clasped Florence's hands and gently scratched the backs with pointy pink nails. "I made stuffed chicken divan," she said, and Florence noted a straight row of Cheerio-sized teeth.

Roy looked wind-tousled, hair an inch past the ears, shoulder blades arching with nerves.

"Aren't you going to hug me?" Florence asked him.

Instead, he presented the casserole dish filled with well-cooked chicken and cheese. She took it. "You look well, son."

Jim shook Roy's hand. "I assume the drive was good." He removed Parliaments from his jacket pocket. "Got your favorites."

Julie *ooh-aah*ed the tea roses growing around the chimney stack while the men smoked. David John came out and flicked the rubber lasso over the landing. "Hullo, sis."

Julie gasped. "You're David John!"

"Yes." He flicked his rope like a snake tongue.

"And where are my other new siblings?"

"Vera will be back for dinner, and Lora is Daisy Mae in the high school parade."

"Your sister is in a parade?"

David John turned a devil's eye on Florence. "It's Sadie Hawkins. Not for married people." He flung the lasso at Julie's ankle.

Roy picked him up. "Watch it, Crockett. You hear?"

David John head-butted Roy. “Make us go to the parade! Please?”

Julie pulled her skirt down. “Could we go inside? I’m cold!” Without waiting for an answer, she led the way to the kitchen, guessing at where it was, and put her dish in the cold oven. Time was moving too fast for Florence to keep up, so she said nothing and situated herself in the corner of the kitchen, and tried to accept that they would be eating this simple casserole. She instructed the daughter-in-law to plate Vera’s vegetables, too, just as Roy came in and went to his echo’s framed fan in the hall.

“We’re about to eat,” Florence said.

He stared at the beaded handle and the dyed orange and blue eagle feathers.

Julie stopped plating. “Roy says you come from a chief? Your ancestors must’ve been noble.”

Florence wanted to yell, or at least scold, but Jim came in and pinched her hip, signaling to let it go. She scooted into the kitchenette booth and bit her tongue, watching her husband crinkle his cheeks into that salesman smile with a side glance at her that pretended they were both just actors in a movie. Julie giggled and took a seat across from him.

His smile deepened. “On our first date, I ordered Florence a gin and tonic, not knowing she doesn’t drink. She said it smelled like juniper, drank it to be polite, and then she told me her ancestry. I couldn’t believe it.” Jim sat back, dragged on his cigarette, and blew some smoke in Julie’s face. He crossed his long legs and cocked his head. “It’s just one of those things.”

Meanwhile, Roy drifted farther into the dark hall, stopping in front of a black-and-white picture. Florence knew which one it was. He’d always lamented what he had never known: a departed grandmother, a nonexistent father. His silence made the air heavy as he returned to the table and joined them, finally. Florence could feel Roy forming the question, once again. The one that always came up. Stiffening, she looked to her daughter-in-law, expecting interrogation, but Julie folded her hands in the posture of confession. "Roy and I have news."

Florence covered her mouth without realizing it. "You're not?"

Julie giggled toward the ceiling. "I am!"

Jim put his cigarette out on a tea plate in the center of the table. "Well. Who could top this? I'm married and now there's a new one coming into the family. Congratulations."

"Thank you," Roy said to Jim, his tone an inch short of *You're not my father*. He dragged a hand over his brow so that his hair appeared to recede. "And, Mother, my wife might like to know. Just how Indian will the baby be?"

Julie put a cigarette in her mouth and asked Roy to light it. Both of their chins turned orange from the lighter and Florence remembered the term for *orange,* ze zhutse eko^, meaning "red and yellow mixed," like that. Roy watched Florence from the corner of his eye.

"If you're asking about the baby's blood quantum, my mother was a quarter-blood, my echo is a quarter-blood, her echo was a half-breed, and her echo was the daughter of Chief Pawhuska. He's Indian, and any children you have will be Indian."

Julie got up and nodded with a flounce of her skirt, then opened the oven. With the oven mitts she'd already discovered herself, she took out the casserole and dabbed the gelatinous fat in her rubber chicken dinner. Jim dusted off his hands and asked Roy how he'd proposed. Florence didn't hear the answer over the sound of David John entreating Julie to watch his skip jumps, which she promised to do after dinner. It was irritating, to say the least, that this young woman had effortlessly taken over the preparation of dinner in Florence's own home, and she escaped to the dining room to find matches on the china cabinet, which she then used to light six blue candles on the table candelabra centerpiece in an act of defeat signaling she'd been reduced to aesthetics.

Julie relocated their drinks from the kitchenette to the fully set dining room table, and they all sat. Florence said a blessing, which Jim tolerated in open-eyed silence. Everyone ate without speaking until Julie asked if the girls would be joining.

"I'll go get Vera!" David John scooted his chair back, eager to move.

"No. Sit. They'll be in," said Florence. "They know what time dinner is."

Florence chewed twenty-six times, to ensure proper digestion. It would all be fine.

Jim and Roy talked about football and work. Florence found herself telling David John to go take his bath, so that he'd set the house into a whir of hot-water pipes and drown them all out. Later, once everyone was finished and David John had bolted off, Jim suggested he and Roy move into the living room, closing the French doors as Julie and Florence cleared plates. Through the divided panes of glass, Florence watched them open a box of chocolates. They wanted to be untouchable, a silent movie in Technicolor, but Florence knew they were cowards. Roy lifted a chocolate to his lips and Jim arranged logs in a tripod over a pile of smoking newspaper. Fool men, oblivious, caring only for food, comfort, control. Tonight, they deserved exactly none of it. Too late, the pipes shuddered overhead as David John started his bath.

She removed the clip from her twist, pulled curled tendrils around her shoulders, and pushed open the French doors with her toe. Roy settled farther back into her favorite toile chair beside the fire as Florence pinned him with her eyes. "I'm ready to tell you. What you came for."

Jim deposited a round chocolate back into the box. "What are we talking about?"

Ignoring him, Florence took a step closer to Roy. "You're an adult. It's time, I suppose."

Roy folded his arms tight around his middle.

The fire settled in its first break. A twinge curled in the middle of her head, as though her brain were rearranging itself; she fell silent.

Roy stood. "Please, Mother. We're here all the way from Texas. Just be polite."

"Why did you move so far away in the first place? Just to get away from me?" Wood popped in the fire, and the fallen picture by the mantel caught her eye.

"That's it. I'm not doing this."

"Wait," Florence said. "I promise, I'll tell you. Just sit."

In the dining room, Julie was blowing out the candles, smoke encircling her like a halo.

"Julie," Roy said. His voice rang loud in the house.

She passed through the French doors and took Roy's hand.

Florence sat down on a corner of the red couch. Her body felt instantly small, as if she were shrinking in that very moment. If they made it all the way to the door, she might disappear.

"I'll tell you if you'll just stay," she said.

Roy turned to Julie, and they agreed to something silently.

"Jean. His name is Jean."

"Jean who?" said Roy.

"Tallman."

Julie and Roy sat in the chairs opposite Florence. "Tell me about him," said Roy.

"He was my tenth-grade teacher. I never told you, because he hit me. When I told him I was pregnant with you." Florence could remember the feel of Jean's hands on her, and the bark of the tree against her back, body with a feeling like obliteration, and the explosion of stars, until she was bruised by the rub and slide of right and wrong every night of her sixteenth winter. "I realize now that he took advantage of me. Aunt Cherie kicked me out. When I told him about you, he gave me pills to end it. I wouldn't take them, so he hit me."

Julie's face was blank as a doe's. Roy stood, but he was so flustered he lost his balance and knocked the chocolates off the side table. A cherry cordial fell onto the picture of her son.

"Can't we all just be happy?" Julie pleaded.

Florence turned back to Roy. "If you can't feel that winter in your blood, there's not much else I can say to you."

Julie moved to the edge of Roy's chair. "Should we go check in somewhere?"

Florence shut her eyes, willing Lora to come home, act the Daisy Mae, and flirt. Even prudish Vera would be a help in this situation, with her pained aims at the art of conversation.

She could hear Roy getting his keys from the entry table.

"Don't go! I'll make up the sofa. I can make coffee. There's fresh pie; Lora made it." Florence's eyes filled with tears. "You have to stay until Lora comes home, at least. Please."

Roy opened the front door and cold air rushed in, along with Vera, holding the mail.

The red font of the BIA quarterly check matched the roses on her blue cotton dress.

"Bonsoir. Je rentre. Good evening. You must be Julie?" Vera extended a slim, icy hand to Julie, who complimented her dress and asked if she wanted a ride around the block in their car.

David John came out in pajamas. "Are y'all going driving? Roy, will you drive us out to Okesa? Then we can get some Indian paint pod that Lora won't get me and play cowboys and Indians with face paint, but I don't want to be the cowboy—you do it, Roy."

"Enough," said Roy. "We're going. Vera, it's nice to see you."

"Going where?" Lora crested the porch steps in singsong. When she saw Julie, she laughed. Julie reciprocated and they embraced like long-lost sisters. Vera stepped back like an interrupting acquaintance, and David John groaned. "Let me in!" he said.

Lora gave David John a quick squeeze and then picked him up.

"How was the parade?" Julie asked.

"Good," Lora said. From the pocket of her skirt she took a small brown rock with blooming, bulbous knobs on it and offered it to David John.

"My paint pod! Where did you get it?"

"That boy from the football team finally went fishing out on that creek back there." She turned to Julie. "Our ancestors used to break it open and use the powder in here for face paint."

"How exotic!" Julie said.

David John offered the rock to Roy, but he ignored it. Julie clutched Roy's hand like she was afraid of them all. And Roy, he looked hurt.

"I'll boil water for tea," Florence offered. Roy nodded, so she went, but as soon as she left them, Julie began talking, free and easy. Roy said something about the Phillips Mansion, and everyone erupted in laughter. Florence didn't even know what they were talking about. Why had it become a real party the second she'd left? David John followed her into the kitchen and begged her to allow him to try coffee, but she said nothing.

Vera came up behind him, and David John drew an invisible arrow from an imagined quiver and strung it back. "Your chicken was burned! But don't worry. You smell good. How are you so shiny? Shiny, and doing nothing."

Vera started lecturing him. "I did all your jobs today, DJ. Why are you even awake?"

Florence gripped the sink and ignored them. She needed to think of something happy. Jim had told her that morning, while she stood over the same sink, that she was like the best mood of his life; warm weather making a second spring at the end of fall. She'd had no idea he was so poetic. They could be a better family with new ways, she thought as she watched Vera cut the pie. A moment later, Lora came in to help plate it, with David John suggesting different-sized forks and napkins and a kind of tea that Florence didn't have. None of them knew that she had been looking for David John all afternoon, racing the sun, combing the neighborhood, spitting into the creek that was her life until it became a goddamn waterfall. She wanted them to get out of the kitchen.

Then she remembered Roy and Julie. "Are my children staying?" she said.

"They went outside with Jim," Lora said. "Can we eat in bed? I need to study."

Florence didn't answer. An engine hummed from the street. She rushed to the porch as Roy was backing out, staring at the rearview like there was nothing else in the world. The ground seemed to pull at Florence. She had to grip the window frame, but Jim grabbed her around the waist, turned her, and held her face to his. She touched his head carefully, like a pot on a clay spinner, and let him pick her up, hands pressing her into a tighter, more manageable self, one that held together and fit him. He took her into the house, and she hoped the children would see that she had a good man, but they had already retreated to their rooms. It seemed to take only a second before she and Jim were in their own, too. He was pushing his mouth onto hers and put her on the bed and she let him struggle off every bit of her clothing down to her stockings, still caked with the blood from David John's portrait. Jim's kissing was as cool and quiet as a swim in a cold pond and she cried because she wanted him. When they separated, her lips opened and she slept with the old dream of her mother's funeral, burrowing under trade blankets to the sound of Echo's talk, the blankets tying her between her dreams and life.

BY ALCATRAZ

Mary places her patterned Minnetonkas beside Daren's white sneakers, a brand she doesn't know. The entryway is so small that she has to sidle up the steps to not touch his hip as he slides inside and locks the door.

"So you really don't celebrate Thanksgiving?" he says.

She follows him up the dusty staircase, and his narrow hips in khaki remind her of her high school crush. "My grandma says Thanksgiving is a PR stunt, and we can't celebrate."

"PR stunt like how?" says Daren.

Mary tries to think of ways to explain as they go into the kitchen and he invites her to sit. Why does she have to explain this? Daren is lifting a French press, offering her coffee. Before she can answer, he says, "Anyway, Friendsgiving is different, at least I hope." He pushes the top of the contraption and pours the liquid into two glass mugs.

The coffee he gives her is the perfect temperature and when she drinks it her body feels warm, almost too warm, like she's angry or panicked or embarrassed but doesn't know which. So far, this day isn't going great. She's felt disoriented since she woke to Daren's selfie text.

He is putting on a record of some type of prog rock. "So what were you trying to get a photo of, walking around the city?" he asks, just as Mary proclaims: "I like sweet potatoes." *Oh my god*, she thinks. What an idiotic comment. "In terms of Thanksgiving foods," she adds.

He saves her from having to say anything else by announcing he will boil more water for more coffee. She likes him, a little. How he's betrayed himself in having admitted, albeit mistakenly, that he saw her walking around taking pictures in front of the library. Meaning the selfie he'd sent that morning paired with the words *hang later?* could have been a response to a semicreepy moment during a lone, wandering drive around campus. Daren pushes floppy, silky hair behind his ears and smiles in a spaced-out way. He looks tired, too. Maybe they are the same, she tells herself, two regular people trying awkwardly to stay alive. She wants to hug him.

Finished with the kettle, he puts on a new record, this one less upbeat. It's like her lo-fi hip-hop channel in that it's calm, but it's more droning, maybe like what house music is, though she isn't sure. Anyhow, it seems like study music, and makes her blush at the back of Daren's khaki pants and dark blue tee made of a nice, thick material, thinking how this time of the week they would usually be sitting next to each other in their sociology lecture and she'd be checking out his sneakers, he'd bring her Starbucks. Here they are, as usual: drinking coffee, exchanging almost-funny-but-not-quite remarks instead of notes written in the same vein.

Daren pours the coffee into a little glass pourover top this time, and he brings it over to the table so she can watch. It's like he knows she doesn't know about the same stuff as him. He's sitting close to her, and she can catch his soap / fresh-wheat smell. Between pours, he looks her in the eyes and she doesn't know if they are going to kiss. When he pours again, her cup is full, so she sets the pourover thing on a plate and picks up the mug and holds it in front of her face to shield herself, but he is making eye contact. Does he not know it's disrespectful and forward?

He cocks his head, an attempt at cuteness. Or maybe trying to break the weird tension of the moment, or else waiting for her to try a conversation topic of her own. About photography? She barely knows anything about it but point and shoot. She could try Thanksgiving again.

"The Thanksgiving thing, well. It's like the marketing by oil companies that we looked at in that case study. Shell starts a STEM school for five hundred orphans to distract from an oil spill. In our case—I mean, Natives'—government and companies and history books have turned it into a bucolic feast celebrating generosity, but it was a mass poisoning. Shouldn't you know?"

"Oh, right, of course. And sorry, I didn't realize you were Indian. I mean, Native."

Fuck. Way to ruin the moment. "What'd you think I was?"

"Um, uh, mixed?"

She looks at the grainy wood of the table. Her grandmother's advice comes to her: *Try to place it easy on yourself.* She downs her coffee and tries again, responding to his other question.

"I was working on a self-portrait with nature and cityscape for a painting."

Daren opens the fridge and removes a huge turkey, stuffed and tied, which he presents in her direction. "Almost forgot! It's time."

She compliments his work, and notices the oven is already on. It is impressive, but also boring. As Daren lowers his bird into the oven, she takes a moment to get her bearings. It is safe here, and it feels oddly safer to her than being alone. The house is tidy but old and dusty. The voice of her grandmother in her head says: *Make friends, you're getting creepy.*

She slept through her other friend-making option for the day, the sunrise ceremony on Alcatraz; not entirely her fault since there aren't any other Native students she knows at her own school to go with her. If her grandmother were still around, she would go home. There is nowhere else to go except to try to contact an auntie she barely talks with in Oklahoma. She refocuses on Daren, who is saying how it's chilly and putting on a black hoodie that has a kind of sheen, like it's covered in Scotchgard. The turkey is in the oven, and her host flips his vinyl over.

"So," she says as Daren comes back in and leans against the counter. "Where are you from originally?"

"My family is from Southern California, but I went to boarding school here in the city."

"Oh. So, would that be, like, England?"

He looks kind of freaked out. "Oh, hm. I don't really know much about that stuff."

"Oh, sorry," says Mary. "Well, my grandma went to a boarding school, too. But I think it was pretty different."

"We both must've known the feeling of not having family around."

She nods. They can agree on that.

Daren seems smart and sensitive. Her grandmother was right to tell her to come here.

"The boarding school was my idea. I loved it, overall. I mean, look. I'm here!" he says, and gestures toward the apartment. The floorboards creak when he comes back to sit beside her, as though in agreement. "There's so much mood in this city. Is this your city, too?" he asks.

"I'm from out east, but my grandmother came here for the occupation of Alcatraz and never left."

A door slams and a pronounced *WOOO!* travels from the living room. Mary jumps in her seat, but Daren doesn't seem to take notice.

"Ah, you need another refill. Or switch to wine?"

"Wine?" She doesn't drink. Hasn't ever drank. The realization that Daren could've put something in the coffee is too much. She can't think of what to say. There is the sound of footsteps on the stairs, and she listens with a dead feeling in her chest. "I think somebody's home," she says.

"I was wondering when they'd turn up," Daren mutters.

She can tell he's disappointed. "What is it?"

"My roommates."

"For Friendsgiving?"

He nods. "I guess we'll meet them. They've been out on one of their 'club' adventures."

"Club?" Mary breaks into a chuckle.

"They have a *club*." He raises his right hand and twirls it as if holding a wand.

"Are they…wizards?" She laughs again, and Daren laughs, too.

"No, warlocks. J-k, but they definitely act like they're something else."

Why is he not part of the club, she wonders, without asking. He changes the music again. Back to the first record. She's grateful to hear the sounds; it's something familiar as Daren chops an onion while moving his hips, and the room goes wobbly. For a moment, she isn't sure what's happening, but the sight of her empty mug reminds her. He put something in her coffee.

It makes her think of sophomore year in high school, when her crush Sam Weathers was always trying to get her to try drugs. Her biology partner from the tenth grade, he was the one guy in high school she'd liked. Not just because he was Nansemond and she was Wazhazhe. Sam was funny, and thought Mary was funny, and they wrote each other jokes while the young teacher directed the lesson at the girl in their class he was secretly dating. Sam Weathers helped Mary take the daily focus off creepy. But he also asked her to smoke behind the gym, illegal stuff, and she hated the thought of her grandmother finding out. Drugs were the supposed reason she didn't have parents. They were homeless or else hiding out somewhere in Tulsa. Was this feeling what had taken her parents away? Her mug is still there on the table, looking somehow guilty. She is ready to leave, and she plans to stand quietly and slip out, but when she tries she knocks Daren's chair and almost falls.

His eyes are wide open. He seems paused, like a person in a video.

"I really need to powder my nose," she says. It's something she's heard her grandmother say, and although it sounds absurd here and now, he can't read her tone, and his confusion makes her feel like she has the upper hand. The indie music ends, and the needle skips over the end of the vinyl. Daren smiles at her weirdly, incoherently, and he points her across the hall into a clean room with two doors and a little tea candle burning quaintly on the back of the toilet.

As soon as she closes the door, laughter sounds through the other door, then stops.

Something in her wants to cry. She visualizes the hem of Daren's pants, folded with crispness. Preppy, but not when paired with the hoodie. Were the roommates off-kilter preps? Why hadn't they come into the kitchen to say hello? She steps carefully out of the bathroom and heads down the hallway. She's going to leave. But before she can, a door flies wide open and a white carpeted room flashes into view, with kids she feels like she's seen before, at one of the concerts at the venue down the street, where she sits in the corner alone, pretending to read a book to redirect the sad girl impression to loner-intellectual. One of the kids is wearing tons of black rubber bands as bracelets on her thin wrists. They move like Slinkys up her arm.

"Hi," she says.

"Hi," says Mary. She couldn't guess the race of her interlocutor by phenotype, but many tiny braids signal that she's in the category of Black, which makes Mary think that she should be doing something more in the way of presentation to signal that she is Native. But what can she do that isn't totally offensive to herself? If she wore her hair in a left side part with a silk bow, that would be Wazhazhe, but no one would know. Or she could be like 1920s Wazhazhe people wanting to be recognizable to I^shdaxi^, wearing beaded headbands over her forehead in the popular stereotype of the time. Those old photos always bothered her, and she stares at her bare feet. She is standing on a "Native-inspired" rug, probably from a big box store, not Native-designed or made—as she knows the law requires—but appropriated.

Another girl interprets her silence as shyness, and intervenes. "Daren, introductions?" She has a somewhat thin face, and sits shuffling a deck of cards on an upside-down milk carton. Mary notices her Care Bears shirt and her very long, very curly hair done into two excellent, tight Native-style French braids.

Daren speaks. "Sorry, this is my date."

"Date?" The girl with rubber band bracelets looks over as she picks up a VHS and removes it from its sleeve.

"*Date?*" Mary repeats. She had thought this was a hangout.

"Sorry—Friendsgiving date," Daren apologizes again, and points at the Care Bears girl. "This is Darla." Then he points at the bracelets girl. "And that's Joy. So will you guys wanna eat soon?" Mary cannot believe he's pointing right at people. She would never say yes to a date.

"Eat maybe in like thirty" A third kid with a deep voice says this, and Mary has to step into the room to see him sitting in a bean bag in the far corner.

Joy turns from the video machine. "Hey. You wanna watch *Blade Runner*?"

Bean Bagger grunts. "No. They are not initiates." He is the same light brown as Mary's dad in pictures from the eighties.

Mary waves at him. "Hi, to you, too," she says. "I didn't see you before. I'm Mary."

"Latif." He nods.

Joy says, "So Latif's noting that *this* is the Broken Persons' Club. Are you a broken person? I ask because technically we're a club, and you'd have to be a broken person to watch the movie…"

Mary thinks of not having parents but having a grandmother, until recently. Still, she answers: "No?"

Joy inserts the VHS and presses buttons on the machine. "So why aren't you at home?"

It's a good question Mary doesn't want to answer. "Nowhere to go, at this time," she says. Then she laughs, because it sounds like her idea of a business email or a PR lie. *At this time.*

Ms. Braceleted Tiny Braids VHS Joy looks at Mary like she is crazy, then says, "Same."

Mary turns to Daren. "I guess I should've asked the same of you, huh?" Before he can answer, a random wave of extreme sleepiness overwhelms her. Eyelids closing.

Darla jumps up and catches Mary.

"Thanks," Mary mumbles.

As Darla steadies her, Mary considers her possible indigeneity. It's a weird thing to suspect in this moment, but they both have those old-fashioned names and the habit of braiding their hair so tight it hurts.

"So do *you* want to watch *Blade Runner*?" Darla tries. Her dark brown nose wrinkles as she guides Mary to a bean bag. "If you want to watch *Blade Runner*, just try and share one reason you are quote, broken."

"Maybe if she's joining, I should join," Daren suggests, to which all are silent. Mary finds herself averting her eyes in embarrassment, and then Daren leaves quickly, saying he has to tend to the food. Joy relaxes against the armoire holding the TV and draws her legs in close. "It would be better if you share how you broke recently, or how you are broken now."

Mary nods. She knows they are going to judge her by what she says, and she wants friends who are selective and protective, so she focuses on finding the right words.

"What I hate most in the whole wide world right now is I feel like I live in a different country that's here, inside this one, but no one believes my country exists."

Daren comes back in, and she speaks while looking at him. "I look white, but I'd be lying if I say that's what I am. It's quite a pickle," she says.

"I was just coming in to say that hors d'oeuvres are out in the kitchen."

Darla ignores this. "You can watch *Blade Runner*. But not you, Daren, unless you up and tell your secret, too. We're not even about this colonial holiday, but—we do need to eat."

Daren unzips his black hoodie and remains expressionless. He is wearing blue. The reveal of the blue shirt under the hoodie feels like a moment of vulnerability. But this thought, that Daren's clothes *are* his emotions, is just too dumb, and Mary cracks herself up. As the giggles come, she steps past Daren and rushes into the hall so the group won't think she is weird. Daren is saying something to them, but she can't hear what.

Latif follows her to the kitchen and says he's going to make himself a plate. Mary focuses on walking, but almost knocks into the chair for the second time that day.

"Are you alright? You seem…dizzy?"

Mary *is* dizzy. She shakes her head. "I kind of want to leave. I think Daren spiked my drink and I do not drink," she says.

"That's not cool." He gives her a good look. "We can make sure you're not alone with him? If you want. He's kind of oblivious. I don't think he meant anything by it, but even so."

Latif's emphasis on safety makes her eyes water. She starts making her own plate so he won't see her cry. Being alone in this city by the freezing, desolate Pacific with its sneaker waves and continual gusts makes her feel generally afraid.

"Thank you," she says. "Yes."

He sits down and texts for a minute as she plates. "So. Where did you and Daren meet?"

"We're study buddies. Just in sociology lecture together. He brings me coffee."

Everyone else approaches the kitchen, and Mary goes quiet.

"Oh my gosh! Daren cracked!" It's Joy speaking, rubber bands tumbling up and down her arms as she talks. Mary manages to land her plate on the table and close her not-leaking eyes while the rest of the group compliments the spread and fills Latif in on the secret Daren has apparently just felt ready to spill. She can't follow exactly, but it's something about a botched inheritance. They decide on watching *Blade Runner* while they eat. When Mary tries to stand, Joy, who's just been checking her phone, spots her and winks.

Latif texted, Joy mouths, while Daren grabs her plate with a semichivalric flourish. "Allow me!" he says, and then rushes to the other room to find them seats.

Joy whispers, "We would never have lived with him, it was a last-minute money thing. But he's all right. You don't look white by the way. You look mixed."

"I'm glad the club is headquartered *here*," Mary manages. "Also, is Darla Native?"

Joy looks shocked for a moment, then laughs. "Don't you know most Black people are mixed? I'm half white."

"Oh, no. I thought you guys had more fullbloods."

"You *know* they saved that for the white people!" Joy cries.

They both laugh, until a pang of a headache returns and Mary leans on the wall.

"Powwow in the hall?" Daren approaches to see why they're stalling. "I mean, um, sorry. Forget I said that. Movie's on, and I've got a front row seat if you're down."

Mary wants to tell him not to speak in Ebonics, not even in a watered-down way. Anything, including Old English, would be preferable to that. The appropriation grinds on her, but she just grimaces as she lets him lead her by the fingers into the right-hand seat on a thrift storeish couch covered in old, softened plaid brocade.

"Do you want another drink?"

"What are we drinking?" says Latif.

"Huh? Oh. It's a hot toddy." He turns toward Mary. "It's good, right? Want another?"

"Oh no, no more."

"Daren, what's in your hot toddy?" Latif asks.

"Um, well, it's coffee and whatever liquor you would want in it. I put rum."

"That's not a hot toddy?"

"Sorry," Daren mutters. "I didn't know," he says. He gets up and closes the blinds.

"Didn't know what?" says Latif. "What a hot toddy was, or that Mary doesn't drink?"

Mary feels a burst of energy at this successful confrontation. "Yeah. Which was it?"

"I said 'sorry,'" says Daren. "I didn't mean it like that, I thought people drank…"

"Well, now you *know!*" says Mary. She smiles hugely in the dark before the screen brightens. Today, her goal was to maybe make some friends, and she has done that, besides the fact that she's drugged or drunk. Also, she stood up for herself with some help. The movie title appears in a crazy font, all silvery, and something inside her breaks in a freeing way. Mary doesn't care so much anymore. She watches the movie. The opening scene is complicated and futuristic, and while she can't fully follow, there's a woman with raccoon-like face paint on her who reminds Mary of the Wazhazhe word for *raccoon*, and how it can be associated with a "useless" or purposeless person, which could be a person who can provoke change because they are not in a demanding position. In this situation, she's the raccoon. She changed things.

Throughout the movie, she keeps laughing accidentally out loud at this and other thoughts, like the craziness that I^shdaxi^ brought by leaving their own nations, and then bringing or luring all these other people over to either help them out or claim it was a safe haven. For the first time, she feels that everyone belongs here, on her land, and she's grateful to other people who want to include her and help her, too. She has the notion that she wants to lead them.

After the movie is over, they all go for a walk, and there's a sense that they're the only people in the city, and it's the end of the world. Latif has a film camera, and Mary takes a self-portrait with the timer. It is in nature with a nighttime cityscape in the distance, a flash exposure among trees and with community.

SUPERDRUNK

ᏟᏫᏏᏁᏘᏪᏁ

You have nowhere else to go, he says.
He asks me to say it back to him.
—Raven Leilani, *Luster*

In a teal scoop neck and blue eyeliner, Laney walks into that local bar where Allen Iverson, famous Hampton Roads basketball player, was photographed. She locks eyes with Mark. He is one of the ex-cons on her dad's construction crew, and though he's homeless at the moment, he is not unpaid, so he has chosen this overpriced sports dive for their first date.

He walks over to Laney and, on the way in and out of his hug, she feels his freshly shaven cheek and thinks of the time he invited her to come sleep by him on the job site in his tent. Now he holds her by the flesh of both her arms and charitably offers her a whiskey sour. She accepts and immediately excuses herself to the bathroom. She needs a moment and a mirror to remind herself that hanging out with Mark may be the guilty pleasure of September, but not graduating and therefore not getting away from her dad is the World's #1 Nightmare for life.

In the bathroom mirror, her neatly winged eyeliner confirms she is not yet really drunk; the actual effect of the one drink she had in the car in her coffee mug on the drive over is still uncertain. She is nineteen, almost graduated, and Mark is thirty. Laney goes back out and sips whiskey and tells Mark about acing her AP history test. Mark listens when he wants to argue.

"I just saw this guy I know," he says in response. "I need to go check on him."

Laney is left alone to reflect. Admittedly, she and Mark do have a lot in common (hating her dad, liking to drink, being Native, working construction, enjoying reading). Harm reduction, which Mark practices daily, is not one of those things. As a recovering addict, Mark is focused on helping heroin users use less, or get clean needles, or whatnot. Laney doesn't really know what goes into it. Sometimes Mark talks about reducing harm while they are at the job site at night and he's picking on his guitar and they're staring at the fire, but Laney doesn't do drugs besides alcohol, and doesn't plan to, which is one of the reasons she gets a thrill from hanging out with him.

At the job site, she likes sitting with him under the stars, where it's dark and she doesn't have to talk as much and feel ignored. Now he's still not back and she feels self-conscious not doing anything, so she goes over to the basketball hoop two-pointer arcade game and does a shoot-out with herself on two machines. When she's done, Mark is still talking with the guy, so she leaves. And she doesn't tell anybody else. There is no one else she can even think to tell.

Since she's way out in Hampton, she goes to the Barnes & Noble in the area and reads *Psychology Today* in a leather chair. According to the magazine, the fact that she might be into the idea of Mark trying to manipulate her by not calling or paying attention to her on a date means she may suffer from a "weak sense of self." Still, it feels like affection to her: all that effort to control her. Maybe next time she'll wait around and then say yes to drinking all night.

A man, about forty-five years old, walks up and asks if he can buy her a coffee.

She shuts the magazine firmly. "I have a deadline."

This is something she imagines a journalist might say, and she is wearing the Editor Pant from New York & Company, which was on sale for $19.99. The man nods but doesn't leave, so she does, striding out of the store in her Editor Pant. Back in her work truck, she goggles *weak sense of self manipulator.* There is one article of interest: "Boys Love Girls with Daddy Issues." She doesn't click. No one needs to tell her that her issues boil down to her dad making her work at his construction business, with a crew of guys who are fresh out of jail or have suspended licenses or have otherwise *made mistakes*. She's begged and bargained to bring in money through a Realtor's assistant job she's been offered, but his response to this is to ignore her, hit her, or yell. All that matters is that she does whatever he wants, like going into Lowe's so the men will load the truck for her and her father can save labor costs. He also likes to buy her dresses and take her camping and do other things her mom won't do. She thinks about this and cries as she drives home on Route 460, where the truckers fall asleep and nosedive into rainwater ditches before they can rip the corn and peanut and cotton fields to pieces.

The next morning on the way to school, Laney stops at the bank off Route 460 and finds Mark's note in their brick, the loose one under the monument in the middle of the city square. The note is dated *Monday 1:11 a.m.* In it, Mark points out first that he was drunk at the time of writing, after spending the night at the bar talking with a Portsmouth bookstore manager after she *ditched*. It says he wants to tell her the whole story of meeting the bookstore manager, but he doesn't. It's a ploy to keep her *waiting* on him. This is what manipulative types do, or that's what she got from the Internet articles. *Fuck him*, thinks Laney. After school, she could go to the Mexican joint where they don't card and get drunk enough to go catch him sleeping on the lot with a fire he hasn't put out, save him from flames, then maybe they'd kiss. But she has to cook.

The note goes with her to school. If Laney is being truthful, she is relieved she is not having sex behind the mall with boys like her friend Railene. She hasn't even kissed Mark yet; mostly because Laney is motivated *not* to have sex, understanding that sex = pregnancy = marriage = "I own you!" = no Editor Pant striding through New York City. Still, while Laney is not talking to Mark, she has a stomachache and can't breathe and sometimes has to excuse herself from class. Her mom took her to the doctor about the breathing issue, but he said it was nothing. From what she's read online, he should offer to prescribe her anti-anxiety medication, but doctors in this part of the South don't believe in any mind-body link, or else they don't care.

Saturday arrives. In the cold light of an 8 a.m. job site, Mark is the kind of "hungover" that means *still drunk*. This restoration apartment job is in a sort of bad part of town, and she is alone with Mark and two plasterers. Laney's dad has ordered her to clean the hallway and the stairs, and the plasterers keep brushing their bare calves against her arms on their march up and down the small 1880s house. Little purple and green dots swarm her vision in brief blackouts. Inside these glimpses of nothingness, the desire to have sex with Mark is born. She rationalizes: They are both sad, smart, and hopeless. His ideas are new: atheist science, benefits of weed, construction beer. They are both not special people. It must be normal to feel this connection. At lunch break, they go for burgers at the Portsmouth Café across the street, and she tells him how her mom drank crème de menthes at fourteen until she found Jesus and now she parrots Laney's dad and works at his business. Her point is that she feels unable to find meaning, stuck between the two poles of existence in her parents' world: sin and spirituality. Mark has the same kind of stories to tell. That's maybe the appeal with him. He seems to get what she's going through. And it's fun to be out of place at the nice spot in the neighborhood, a café crowded with mirrors and dated nineties New Age art.

Laney orders a giant piece of chocolate cake as Mark tells a story about the permanent hearing loss in his left ear from a gunshot and a dad who punched him often. She feels safe right now, imagining Mark having sex with her, with a gun nearby. This scenario would create a change in her relationship with her dad, because her dad gets and sees other Oklahoma Indians in a way he does not get or see anything or anyone else. Laney dips cake in coffee and bounces in her seat and imagines herself on Halloween standing in a four-directional breeze dressed as Lady Liberty.

She tells Mark about going to Oklahoma in the summers to see the only person in her family who doesn't need anything from her. Her grandma. There, Laney gets lemon cake from the grocery store, Turner Classic Movies, and tea. It is extremely clean, and she goes there when her dad is at the men's church retreat. Grandma told her the trick with men is to kiss them with your lips parted and your head tilted sideways. Mark seems impressed with this.

Back on the job site the rain comes down like blue gems. There is no kiss yet, but Laney's blood feels magical as it flows through her body, sparkly inside her veins, which is probably from the cake and coffee. At some point, he refers to her as the Prairie Princess and she leaves early, visualizing herself screaming with her dad for hours about not working, if that's what he wants. She would be in huge trouble for leaving early, but for some reason she doesn't care. He is out "driving around," Mom says when she gets home. Instead Laney vacuums, makes mashed potatoes, scrubs the bathroom, then goes to her room and draws a picture of a shoe.

Under the shoe she writes, *do or DYE,* then a series of puns and one-liner stories of people who dye things. It's not a proper story, it's more of an abstract piece. She worries she will not be able to become a proper writer, doing this type of thing, but the wordplay calms her:

At the end of the world, we were all relieved, because we were all dying together.

She falls asleep until 8 p.m., when her door lodges open. He is in the doorway. He is looking at the drawing on her desk. She says nothing as he moves to sit on the edge of her bed. She can feel him staring at her lips.

"The food you made is good. The mashed potatoes were silky."

The red hibiscus print on her sheets seems to enlarge and then shrink in her vision. "I forgot my algebra homework," she says. "I forgot, and I need to do it now."

She knows why he's there. He's going to ask her to go sneak into the aboveground pool at the neighbors' house. Her breath gets caught in her throat, like when she was in the deep end of the pool at nine, the very first time it happened, and the only way she could breathe was by pushing herself out of the pool and staying there until she was done drip-dropping. He leaves quietly without another word. In bed with her history book, she imagines him sliding through the night on the way to the pool, bats circling overheard, beyond the glare of the streetlamps. She's been having nightmares about being pregnant, smoking, and cockroaches crawling up into her bed and swarming her body.

Later, when she hears her dad come back inside the house after his swim, Laney shuts off the lights in her room and quickly feigns sleep. But she is so tired the sleep becomes real, and she has the worst of her recurring nightmares, the one where construction men corner her in a hidden room in the rectory of a Catholic church and close in on her with creepy smiles. Through a weird window, she sees her mom leaving church with her hand in the back pocket of her own tight jeans, followed by hundreds of other people leaving through the same door as her mom, but no one can see Laney or hear her, and the men keep coming closer. She wakes up weeping, afraid, because she wants to be beautiful for her father and it's shameful. He is always watching and wants her, and this twisted attention with an edge of danger—it's the only kind she is ever going to get. She goes back to bed and dreams of having sex with him, then killing him. It's 6 a.m. when she wakes up to scramble eggs, and her mom asks for a scrambled egg sandwich. Her dad hears the order and quickly comes down to ask for one, too.

Laney nods, and he shoves her teasingly. She refuses to budge. "You have impeccable balance," he says. "Always have."

"Doesn't mean people aren't always trying to knock me over."

Her mom stops in the middle of the kitchen. "Do not disrespect your father."

Dad laughs, shrugs, shows his big teeth as he says, "Doesn't matter. Give me a hug."

I'm not your mother, she wants to say, *or your cousin, sister, girlfriend, whatever*. But if she says *Whatever*, or even worse, *No*, she will be punished. She turns the heat up, then accepts the embrace.

After class, Laney and Railene take themselves to the county fair. They eat cotton candy and drink Diet Coke and it makes them not feel like shit. Railene says she is still having sex behind the mall with the guy she is dating and Laney admits she still has a crush on Mark but has done nothing about it. Then she confides that when they go on trips together, just her dad and Laney—road trips through small towns where they stay in motels and sleep in the same bed—she is terrified. Is this how great writers are made? Invariably he asks her to lie on him, hug him, touch him. Predictable as always, Railene thinks that Laney should keep dating Mark and move out from her dad's as soon as humanly possible.

The fair empties out, and the girls part, Laney to her truck and Railene to an old Mustang. At home, Laney does worksheets on the Internet to help with the "weak sense of self." She takes a long run on the treadmill and goes to bed sweaty. She wakes and dresses for class and plays loud music on her drive and attends school. Mark calls between geometry and study hall, at 11:52 a.m. It is Wednesday. When she answers, and says hi, he laughs. It's a big, free laugh.

"What?" Laney says. She laughs back but she's full of nerves.

"I actually lost your number but I somehow remembered it anyway," says Mark.

"You must be good with numbers."

"Yeah, I am good with numbers. And your number has a nice logic to it, too." Laney feels repulsed (why?) and says she needs to go.

He calls her back after school, as she's walking through town.

"It's actually my birthday," he says. "I'm thirty-one."

"Oh. How do you feel about that?"

Mark starts talking and she goes through the STOP acronym, to check the tendencies that may make her attractive to Mark if he is a manipulator type. Her fear of conflict, desire to please, and her inability to enforce boundaries. The acronym goes: "Stop: What do I really want here?...What can I do to move Toward that?..." She forgets what the other two letters, *O* and *P*, stand for. What Laney really wants is to have someone just try to see her. Like how her dad used to make her feel when she was ten or eleven. He had listened to her (sort of), paid attention (sort of), and wanted desperately for her to think he was interesting (always).

Every old man likes the slim bodies of pre-period girls, she told herself. *It's not that bad.*

Mark is still talking, of course, saying that he feels young and coming up with little examples to prove it. She's embarrassed that she's ignoring him the way her dad mostly ignores her. It feels so impossible to listen to anyone when it feels like no one listens to you. Finally, he asks her about her classes, a boring topic she knows he doesn't care about, but she tries to answer. Still, she wonders as she talks: Why is he a foreman? Why does he even bother to work? He could care less about being there, or about construction. Likely, he would just live at home if he had any family. But she knows the answer: drugs. He's lucky he's stayed out of jail so long, and maybe fear of going back keeps him working, to stay occupied.

"You're breathing hard," Mark says. "Where are you walking?"

"I'm in town. Near our brick."

This reminds Mark of the bookstore manager he met at the bar the other night and he starts telling her about the conversation as she enters the square through its encircling bare-limbed dogwood trees. She walks the crumbling old brick cobblestones carefully, ignoring the monument to a violent forefather Laney doesn't want to recognize. She hates the scene, its whole aesthetic, but she is used to tuning most things out so that her body remains in its manageable equilibrium of hurt, anger, and distraction. She is breathlessly attuned, however, to movement. The thin, swirling breeze that lets her know a storm will be here in a day, and a thin vibration in the sidewalk that tells Laney someone is coming from behind. There is a waft of smoke in the air, too. Not cigarette smoke or weed, but the aroma of burning wood.

The person passes, running, in a blur of red hoodie with hair all over the place like it hasn't been brushed. The girl stops at a spot Laney knows well and turns to face the brick wall of the bank. Laney cannot believe what she is seeing. The girl's backpack is so red, and the wind moves, rushing through the trees, deafening the moment. The girl turns and checks behind her shoulder, and her eyes meet Laney's. They both stare, two lone wolves in a standoff. Laney has lowered the phone, and Mark's voice emits from it weakly as the wind dies down. Laney hangs up as the girl quickly wiggles the brick out, sticks her hand inside the opening to either take something or leave something, and then quickly replaces the brick.

After that she walks away, ignoring Laney, though it's obvious that Laney has caught her. Maybe the girl calculated their vibe of mutuality, and wagers that Laney won't interfere. And the girl is right in that Laney does not want to fight her, but wrong in trusting that she'll leave things alone. The girl begins to run now, like she senses something coming, moving fluidly in her red hoodie and matching backpack, so fast she could be a track runner. Laney does not chase her. Instead, she goes to the brick and takes out the note the girl has delivered to Mark. There is no anger, just curiosity. The psychology magazines would probably say her perverse sense of not-caring and of being empty is a defense mechanism, but to her it's just what *is.* She feels proud of herself for not being bothered by this, and for even getting vaguely turned on by it. Maybe this girl is stalking Mark, she reasons.

She reads the letter. It feels like this message is for her, though she knows it is not. Still, Laney takes a pencil out and scratches out a response to both of them, becoming more conscious as she writes of the fact that she doesn't care what either of them thinks of what she says. The writing is for her, not them. It is to change how she thinks. Finished, she puts the note back and slides the brick into its place-holding spot with the reverence of an effective ritual now complete.

That's it. As soon as she puts it there she can tell that she really doesn't care about anything, and if that is the case, if she is this fearless, she might as well do something with it. She goes home and loads her 1997 Ford Ranger work truck with all her stuff she needs to live while a cat weaves figure eights between her legs. Where are her parents? They are gone, who knows where, and who knows when they'll be back. She gets chills all over and her nose waters, but she keeps packing, shot through with adrenaline. Then all her stuff is in the car and she's speeding away. She feels like Spider, who makes her house wherever she goes. As in the stories, Laney has only to wait, and all things will come to her and break their necks, or in other cases, bloom into her.

BROTHER
𐓷𐓣𐓻𐓪·𐓤𐓘

At Pawhuska he's there again, on the north side of the arbor benches in the hot wind, taking a sip from the water boy's ladle, breathing with two hundred-something dancers in the slowing bells. She passes him as she walks briskly out the north corner of the arbor. He never looks at anyone directly, never speaks to anyone except his uncle and aunt on their bench. He's been to the dances before; she's watched him growing up with her. Always at Pawhuska with his sister, a handsome dancin' Osage, freckled with brown showing through, as her aunt would say.

There are 25,000 Osages on the rolls, and of the maybe 250 in the arbor, he stands out in his cotton-candy-blue silk shirt. This year, she's kind of wanting to meet someone, but what chance does she have with a California boy? His sister's on the bench, also dressed out. She doesn't know their aunt and uncle nearly well enough or she'd go over. She looks at her own clothes. Black silk shirt and red wool skirt. White beads, French braids. And a gaze that divides her face like a knife.

After, his sister packs his regalia. Spoiled. Typical. In a newish Hyundai. They go to Sonic. The place is packed with off-land Osages, everyone in their car, and one couple so lost to meth they drift into the bathroom after asking what day it is and not liking the answers they get. The California siblings don't register this. Sister is aiming a blue straw at Brother's forehead and talking, lecturing. Brother puts Kendrick Lamar on the stereo and the sister keeps talking over it.

He takes the straw from her fingers. On his lips, words that look like: *Please stop.*

She pushes the red order button and asks for a couple of limeades like the Californians.

The dances went late and she has to be up at six to help with cooking at the camp. She's expected, too, for the late meal at her uncle's. The California siblings are receiving their order and paying, and she gets the courage to go over just as red and blue lights cut into the lot with a pitchy whoop. The cop car crowds both of their cars, blocking them and creating a kind of triangle. Brother looks at her, maybe for the first time. She wants to smile but can't. The cop gets out and immediately approaches the Californians. She knows him from her math class in high school. Osage but not cultural. Known hypocrite, arresting people for selling weed while he smokes it, but he's also found some missing persons. He's pestering them, asking what they're doing loitering around here, so far from home.

"Littlesun," she says.

The lights shine on his shaved head as he swivels around.

"Lotta drugs running around here tonight, miss, excuse me." He's gruff but she can tell he recognizes her, though he's struggling to remember her name. "I'm working," he adds.

"They're from here, their license plates just aren't changed yet. They're moving back," she says, and spots their family parked across the way. She nods in their direction. "They're out here dancing."

After asking the Californians for their license and registration, the cop takes a step back and eyes the trunk of the Hyundai, as if trying to make his best guess on whether it's full of regalia or crystal meth. "Don't want no bad medicine," he says with all seriousness.

Sister hands over the registration and it turns out they must still have an Osage family name because he backs off, staring fixedly at the trunk of the car as though it is an oracle.

"Y'all have a good night," and he's off, just as the meth heads stumble out of the bathroom.

"I'm Mina," she says, extending her hand to the brother. He's tall like an old-time Osage. She can't help but like him even more.

"Cyp."

"I like that name."

"Thanks for that, just now."

She shrugs. "I know him." She wants to ask him who his ancestors are, but doesn't.

Intuiting this, his sister introduces herself as Susan, and immediately offers names of their relations, which Mina recognizes. "Out by Okitse?"

"Yeah." Susan refrains from the obsequious smiles I^shdaxi^ needlessly make, instead reaching into the back of the trunk and presenting paint pods.

"What are these?" Mina asks.

Susan gives Mina a brief, hard look, a flash of eye contact. It's obvious she knows. "Why don't you tell me?" she says.

This is the right response, coming from a person whose family left, speaking to one who didn't. There is a power imbalance here, and the fact that this off-land woman knows she needs to respect Mina's family, her residence, and her Indigenous knowledge is proof she can hang.

Mina explains what it is, and how it was used.

"My aunt took us over there today before my brother got in, but she didn't say much." Susan takes a sandwich baggie of dried cedar out from her car door and offers it to Mina.

Mina takes it, impressed. "I appreciate that. So, where in Cali y'all coming from, eshe?"

"Eshe?" says Cyp. So, he's the whiter one.

"Long Beach," says Susan. "Our iko still lives here in Bartlesville and our uncle's here."

Mina is beginning to prefer her to him, but she persists. Conversational ineptitude is not a crime, but she feels her toes clench the foam of her river flops. Water squishes out. "So you're in school, I guess?"

"Engineering. At Stanford."

Stanford. Goddamn.

"Well, you guys could come over for the late meal. You guys are welcome."

The sister takes the Indian paint pod from her brother. "Ready? We need to get going."

"You sure?" Mina asks. She can't help it. These people seem lost as it is.

"It's an old friend. Don't want to let her down."

Cyp pulls out his phone as Susan opens the door to their car. "I'll take your number? In case we stay."

Mina hands her phone over with the text message app open, and he puts his number in and sends himself a message. His phone makes an echoing sound, and he blushes.

"Got it," he says.

"Hey, are you dancing tomorrow?" she asks.

"Definitely."

"Wear purple," she says.

"So you can find me?"

"No." She laughs. "It's Hominy night. People wear purple."

His sister rolls the window down and pokes out a skinny arm. "I have to cook. But I'll look for you out there when I get a break."

"In purple," the brother adds sheepishly. He gets into the car and rolls the window down.

"Kashikada^ iwithe dv mi^kshe."

"…iwithe…?" he asks what he should already know.

"Take a language class sometime. Go on, and be careful." She waves them off and gets back in her own car. There's still a good hour before she has to help clean up from the late meal. She drives to the ranch, but this is a mistake. As soon as she hits the gravel road and crosses the cattle grates, her headlights shine on a dead buffalo. Massive, maggoty, red meat and blood. She cries, a gut reaction, then dials her aunt, who runs the ranch.

"There's a buffalo down out here." She can hear her voice drop and shake. "Where the prairie road connects to town."

"I'm coming," her aunt says. "Be right there."

She remembers the day, just last weekend, when she went to Tulsa for a shawl delivery, how she stepped on a red-black-white-yellow quartered circle, the outline spray-painted green. Osages aren't medicine wheel people, but she thinks of the four sacred colors of the crawfish and how some say the buffalo is associated with one of the corners of the medicine wheel, the side of the earth, or night, and of endings. The most obvious connection is that the animal is dead, and she stepped on the corner of the medicine wheel signifying the west, the time of death. What is dying? Headlights arrive. Her aunt's. She pulls up and gets out, and her boots make a sturdy dull crunch on the road. The sound is comforting.

"How the heck did this guy get out here?" cries her auntie. "We got us a problem."

Her aunt sends her home to help at camp. Mina tells herself she needs to change first at home, but she lies down on the bed just for a moment, and falls right asleep. She dreams. In her dream, she is an accountant at the casino. At a coffee shop, she sits on a high stool with long acrylic nails. Men come in to talk to her but she doesn't acknowledge them because she is out of their league. Then she goes to gamble, using only twenty dollars. An econ prof calls: "This is how the market works. It's not possible to know where it will go. It's gambling."

She wakes at 3:34 a.m. and checks her phone. Nothing. The dream reminds her of Indian dice and hand games. She remembers going to the casino for meal vouchers and the chief in there eating a slice of pizza. He never remembered her name no matter how many times they met. She thinks of her brother, who won't sing or drum anymore, not even for a round dance. Instead he is selling marijuana, an offense for which the cops will put him in jail for years the day they catch him, unless bigger dealers get to him first.

No one texted her about coming to cook. Why not? It seems like a sign that she is clear to text Cyp, who would have had his goddamn car searched had it not been for her. She could type *hey*, just to see what he'll say. Of course, she can't do that. She falls back asleep and dreams again. In this dream, she invites Cyp to eat with her at Sonic but he looks scared, his sister with her head in the passenger-side window of an old Ford talking to a relative. Mina pulls Cyp behind an order board and puts a finger over his lips.

"Ma^ze i^shda," she says, guessing his name.

He nods.

They listen to his sister gossip about Mina as they stand behind the order board. The aunt and the sister say that she, Mina, is sober but used to drink, and that she is not in school and has no job but making traditional clothes. She lives with her mom. The relatives start chattering about a corn-growing conference, and Mina takes a wooden Popsicle stick she's painted yellow and red on one side and black and blue on the other. It's the same colors as the medicine wheel. (Why she's dreaming pan-Indian stuff she doesn't know, but it probably has something to do with city Natives who don't know their ways. Like Cyp.) She becomes conscious, within the dream, that she's dreaming, and begins to direct it. When behind the order board the auntie says, "Y'all know you all need to marry Osage, right?" she wills her and Cyp to go to a party together, but then her phone rings in the dream. It is also ringing in real life. She wakes up and it's a California number.'

"Hello?"

It's Cyp.

"I'm sorry to call you, but there's something going on."

She shakes the sleep away. It's crazy that this is Cyp out of the dream, he's the actual voice on her phone.

"It's okay," she says. Shadows move across her closet door. "What's going on?"

"Well," he whispers, "I'm really sorry, but we're sleeping in my uncle's yard. And my cousin is out here with this Ponca guy, and they won't stop arguing and I know there's nothing we can do..."

That means those two are probably drinking and likely doing drugs, too, which isn't allowed during the dances.

"Say no more. You shouldn't be around that. I'll take y'all to the casino and you can get a room there. You have money, right? And forget cooking tomorrow, bring your uncle over and we'll treat him and all y'all right."

She can almost hear her own smile in her voice as she jumps out of bed. She's dressed, still wearing makeup, and it's 4 a.m. He's still on the line, so he can hear her start the car. She drives toward them and he whispers to his sister. They rustle in their tent and because she knows where his uncle's house is and which side is the driveway, she cuts her headlights so those who are misbehaving don't see her entrance. Sister and brother hustle under the laundry lines and hop in the back of her truck. She's oddly proud of them, how they handle themselves.

"You're Osage," she whispers.

They drive toward the casino with her eye on them in the rearview, moonlight swiped across their faces like silver eyeshadow. She feels free, and thinks on her dreams. The takeaway is that she's attracted to the California Osages. Why? She does want to get out of town. They're stargazing back there, lying low. Maybe because she's taking them with her, some part of her feels like they could take her with them, too? She knows educated Cali Osages now, and wouldn't one of the benefits be a place to stay in California? It would make things far easier.

The image of the buffalo returns to her. A shiver runs through her. In her rearview, she feels like there's something there, but she can't see any lights. It's possible there's a driver with no headlights. Rogue people. Or even their cousin. Her whole body feels clogged with breath as the Ponca casino looms out of the dark like a bursting star. The engine whir beats her heart into a shifting snake and short, random pains stab her with each breath. She hits the turn signal with a rigid hand.

"We're here," she announces, hoping the sound of her own voice will ground her. She turns into a spot, shuts off the engine, and hikes up the parking brake with a click.

She breathes.

"Hey," Cyp says. His voice cools her.

"Go inside," she says. "I think there was someone following us." The siblings hurry out without another word, and she trails behind them. The casino is brightly lit, filled with stragglers smoking and sitting at the buffalo slot machines. Beyond the check-in area are three plush couches beside a water wall feature and a view of the pool. She figures they will feel safe here, and they walk past the front desk and sit down.

The siblings stare at each other for a moment until Susan sighs, shaking her head. "Yes, we can use my card."

Mina thinks of the saying *Find an Osage woman to take care of you* and she wonders if Cyp would want that. Does he like Osage cooking? Would he like how she is in a relationship? Shit, she shouldn't be thinking like this.

"Well, it's really late," she says. The front desk attendant has stepped out to smoke. Out the window, there are eight cars, two of them with people inside of them. One has twins with buzz cuts. The other has a guy with an arm sleeve of tattoos and a girl getting out, wrapped in a Lycra dress and beaded teardrops, borrowing a lighter from teenagers blaring loud music. It's a shift change.

She brought them here because it's the fanciest spot in Osage County, but now she doesn't like how they're standing out, not gambling, not doing anything, not even smoking. She tells them to follow her.

"C'mon. I know a spot that's a bit more chill until you can check in. Afraid of the dark?"

"No." It's Susan who answers.

She takes them off the side entrance of the casino and down the mown lawn toward a pond where lilies grow. Just before the water an owl flies over their path and all three of them stop still. Red-rimmed perfect yellow eyes on a blackjack branch. Feathers splayed on a fat neck.

Susan turns first. "Maybe we should go get that room."

Mina can't argue. She and Cyp follow closely behind until Susan goes to the front desk to check in. They take a seat on the couches. Behind them, the sun is close to rising. It will be getting hot, and Mina imagines the buffalo still out there, flies clicking on the flesh.

Cyp makes a cute humming sound, apparently warming up to start talking. "The other day, I had this weird dream. About this Ponca girl. It was in an airplane, she was sitting in a row of empty seats across the aisle from me. She glowed from the sun, then she got covered in rainbow."

"What do you think it means?"

"I don't know. I was going to ask you."

"Well, what do the colors of the rainbow mean to you?"

"I guess they mean magic, or hope, or something good is coming."

"Then I guess it is. Maybe that's why I saw this buffalo. I saw it earlier today, after I left Sonic's. It was dead in the road. Something's ending, but beginnings come with that usually."

"What's ending?"

"I don't know, maybe one of my lives, so to speak. I think I'm going to have a different life. Maybe I'll go to California."

"Where will you go?"

"I guess I'll apply to school somewhere, or for a job. Maybe L.A. or San Francisco. I heard a lot of Osages went to Brentwood in the twenties. Your great-grandpa probably did that."

"He went to Long Beach."

"Right," she says. She's grinning, she can't stop, and she's leaning a little bit toward him. They're looking at each other, and his eyes move to her mouth. She's thinking that it might happen, that they might kiss, but they hear loud crying behind them.

It's Susan. There's a burst of yells from the casino doors, two men going out punching each other, and the security guards are nowhere to be found. Mina recognizes one of the men from her GED class, her old neighbor who told her last week, "I love you, I want to be your friend. You're my sister." The other guy is a dealer, known for hit-and-runs. It's also known that he's carrying all the time, and a shock goes through her body, a killing rage that weakens her. The message of the owl.

This is how it happens, too quick, and out of nowhere. There is a shot. Her insides turn to magma. She's running, falling, knees skinned, and her friend is on the asphalt feet away. The dealer is sprinting to the car with the twins in it, and it peels away as he dives into the back seat. This isn't supposed to happen here—this is a three-star hotel casino. She wishes for this to be a dream, but the sun is up and it is suddenly so hot. She doesn't know what to do, but she reaches her friend from GED class and drops down beside him, and puts her fingers on his blood. "You are my brother," she tells him.

His eyes are open. "I'm burning up," he says. His hair is braided, soaking in his own fluids, and he is sweating, frown lines crushing his young face. She bursts into tears and begs him not to die. They need him. He is a good singer, and he was learning all the old songs.

"Ha^kazhi^." Mina's body feels cold, though it is hot enough she is now sweating. Tears cover her face, and someone picks up her hand and places a water bottle in her palm. She pours it on her friend as the security guards call the police. Next to her, Cyp and his sister kneel. Mina waves her hands at the moths in the parking-lot brightness of the morning, but they don't pay her any mind. Only a few seconds have passed but she is already resenting the Californians, for having brought her to see this; for being so useless. Then, without warning, Cyp takes off his shirt and he makes a tourniquet.

"Let's not wait anymore We can stop the bleeding, right?" He hands the shirt to her.

The tourniquet seems to work. They help Mina prop the young man's head up and he drinks a little water. The EMTs arrive and take over, but not before he tells Mina to call his mother. She takes his phone and relays what the EMTs are saying, that he is going to the Ponca clinic, and he is lucky it happened this time of day when the EMTs were nearby, and lucky that the bleeding is slowing with the help of the initial tourniquet and now their own. And then she hangs up on the now frantic mother, and the ambulance leaves, and Cyp and Susan and Mina are left alone in the parking lot with the full sun, Tsiko mi^, rising. She talks to the sun in her head, asking for protection, for help, and that they will be kind to each other, and each of them will receive what they need. She dries her eyes and stands.

Cyp stands up, too. "Let's get that room and rest for a while. Stay with us?"

"Yeah, you know, I hear their pancakes here are not bad," says Susan.

Mina laughs, because this girl is reading reviews of casino food. "Okay," she says. "It's a plan." There's no way she'll be able to sleep right now, but if she eats first, who knows?

"This way we're closer to the hospital, if you want to see your friend," says Cyp.

"Yeah, right. Okay. I'm so glad we were here," says Mina. "I'm glad you guys were here."

"Me too," say the siblings.

And they all go back inside together.

A SMALL URGE

ᏁᏍᏁ ᎰᎣ'ᎡᏁ

It is Thursday, the day named after Jupiter, but I am nowhere near jovial. My Lea has just left our walk for a date and I am languishing at the bank of a creek, where I am seated on the stump of an oak. An approaching hiker spots me and waves hello, skirt shimmery with mist, trembling in a breeze, green yarn of her hat bobbing through shreds of lichen. The hiker is dressed well, in leggings and boots. My loafers are soaked clean through and stained with mud.

All this for my Lea.

Earlier, before sunrise, I woke to ready for coffee on the deck of the two-story café in our college town, where I've lived for twelve years. The café is a short distance from my blue stucco encircled in purple rhododendron, and I arrived first on foot. Not seeing her, I pulled out my laptop and set to work on the construction of next semester's syllabus. For this reason, I almost certainly would have missed Lea cresting the wooden staircase of the café deck, bathed in rays of sunlight, had not a greasy crow flapped down to perch on the rain gutters. I saw her, but she did not see me, because she was texting.

"That's a dangerous thing to do," I said, and rose from my Adirondack.

Pills of moisture glinted on her hair, her sweater. She was beautiful. "Priscilla!" she said.

In my arms, she was warm and damp like a fireside skier, and we hugged long in that way that anticipates everything but doesn't know how to begin. As we sat, she glanced at my open computer and pushed her cellular to her jean-clad thigh.

"What are you working on?" she said. "Anything good?"

You see, she likes my stories, little ones I write expressly for her and send in the mail for her to find, genuine surprises among the real estate flyers and credit card offers. She last sent me some old lingerie, as she is getting divorced. I wore the items once before trashing them, and sent her pictures. Strange, I know, but I want to neither hurt her feelings nor be scrambled by the residue of extremely questionable energy on those items.

"Nothing good," I replied, but she reached for the computer anyway. I didn't stop her.

She read from the excerpt of "Walking" by Henry David Thoreau that I'd just copy-and-pasted into the description. "'He would be a poet…who derived his words as often as he used them—transplanted them to his page with earth adhering to their roots.' Love it!"

I loved how she remained so unaffected, and sincere.

"Who else is on the reading list?" she asked.

"Beckett, Genet. You know," I said. "Ofelia Zepeda, Ed Roberson, N. Scott Momaday, Roethke, Natalia Toledo, Camille T. Dungy."

"God." She tilted her head. "That just seems like a lot of writers that people don't know?"

I changed the subject. "I had a dream about you last night."

"Tell me!" she said, but then her phone buzzed on her chair and I was saved. In her year of oscillation between jobs and crushes, the idea of impulsively telling her my own feelings was inadvisable. On her phone, she studied what seemed to be a long-awaited text, probably from the ex-lover she had used to end her marriage to the Americana singer, after too many poorly paying out-of-town gigs had drained her Montessori subbing income and her patience. There was another older dream, also about her. The first dream took place in a Christian retreat hall where we had clandestine sex while a boyfriend or fiancé hunted her down; the second was the older dream, which was set in her ancestors' town of Bratislava, from which she was two generations removed. This is the dream I began to tell her about instead, as her bangs, streaked caramel with store-bought highlights, caught the light. "We're in this decrepit hotel, facing a plaza of disintegrating cobblestones—"

"I'm sorry," she cut me off, and returned her gaze to her phone. "It's John."

I was silent. My silence chided.

"I am sorry."

"Did he say something interesting?"

"Um, not really."

I remained silent.

She arranged her face in a sneer of politesse. "So we're in Slovakia somewhere."

"Bratislava," I repeated. She had never cared much for the details of her own ancestry. "Anyway, we were in an old hotel crowded with antique chandeliers, checkered tile, wall coverings in red, heavy pink taffeta curtains, we sit on a bed with four posts. It begins to rain. You turn into a crocodile, then a frog, alternately. You can turn into either, depending on your mood. And we are looking out on the plaza through the windows where it rains. I regard your amphibious eyes, and ask, 'What does it mean that the Angles, or the Francs, or some tribe crushed another here, metabolizing it, and those people came to our continent and crushed us and we are all crushed underneath this stone?'

"'I don't think these people were Angles, or Francs,' you say, and shrink into your frog self, as you held a needle strung with thread. You shrink small enough that you can enter my bloodstream, and you do, and you swim about inside me and stick the needle into my capillaries."

She paused, imagining that. I was relieved, because she is someone who can be so aloof that she can all but disappear if she dislikes what you say. I did not ask about the text from John, her radio host lover from Chicago. I didn't ask about any kind of drama. Instead, I quoted Claudia Durastanti. Or something I was sure Claudia Durastanti said, about conjuring your own possibilities because no one else will. She giggled, at me, or perhaps at another text. Then she checked her horoscope on an app. After that, we left for our walk in the woods via the footpath across the street. She showed me Tinder dates as we went.

"I'm hoping today's date will be different."

"Today's date?"

"Yes, I'm so sorry. I have to go."

For a moment, I had thought she meant us, now.

It must have showed, because she gave me a snide goodbye kiss, blown off her hand.

"My Lea," I said, trying to return her mocking manner, and in saying it, realized she was not mine at all.

She left me by the tree. A turkey passed, walking daintily as a society woman, and gazed at the shoes Lea has always disliked.

The sky shatters down in an array of droplets and I begin to trudge down the path, but when thunder erupts, I turn and run the other way.

I take shelter back inside the café where we started. I am Scotchgarded head to toe—jeans, duster coat, hat—but the tops of my shoes are open and my feet are wet. The barista eyes me as I place my canvas pack on the chair opposite me at a table for two.

"I'll take a mocha," I tell her.

The barista has a chin sheened with the natural oil of her skin, or maybe moisturizer. I sit and change my soggy shoes for moccasins as she lets the La Marzocco espresso machine hiss. I had stowed the moccs in my bag, as I had originally planned to bead this afternoon.

The barista sets down my mug. "I figured it's for here, in this weather. Cool shoes, by the way."

"Thank you. I made them, and my other ones are ruined."

We study my feet together.

"Not the best choice for a hike," I confirm.

"Yes, your friend was wearing boots, I recall."

I peer up at her from the microfoam as I sip the dark swirls of the frothed milk.

"Hey, if it's not too weird, could I possibly ask you a quick question?"

"Yes," I say. "This is delicious."

She nods with her shiny chin and I realize she wants to sit, so I move my bag from the chair and rest it atop my moccasins with flexed toes, and prepare to listen as she glances at her Mickey Mouse watch face and says that she is off in six hours, to film a dance in this room.

She explains why this is relevant. "I can't decide where to place the third dancer, and I don't know if this is too weird, but I heard you talking about the story of Jupiter before, when your friend was telling you her horoscope? Well, my dance is actually about the three brothers and suns—or sons—of Saturn."

I feel impressed: "Neptune, who was given the sea; his brother Pluto of the underworld; and their third sibling, Jupiter, god of the heavens. How do these folks dance? And why the coffee shop setting?"

"Oh, I figure the coffee shop is where the creative act takes place, and that is what the heavens, earth, and underworld contain."

Impressed again, I quote Duchamp's speech on the creative act. "'Art may be bad, good, or indifferent, but, whatever adjective is used, we must call it art—'"

"'And bad art is still art in the same way that a bad emotion is still an emotion,'" she finishes. I toast her and drain the rest of my mocha as she glances around, both manic and furtive. The only other customer is a boy in the corner tapping rapidly on a cellular.

"Well," I say, "I'm a poetry professor and familiar with the story your dance seeks to evoke, and I have time as I've just been canceled on by an old friend who is either outgrowing me, or I her. It's a shame, but it led me to you, and can that really be a bad thing? Doesn't seem like it. And that boy over there? He won't complain. I know, because he is a neighbor, lives down the street from my house in a modern design of crayon colors. Mustard, hunter green, red. Nice materials, but the design is roughshod as well as pastiche. But I'm getting off track from my point, which is that he should be happy today, what with the rain. Usually his mom scolds him to play outside, but now he has an excuse to stop his walk at the quarter-mile mark, and it's because of the rain. I'm talking to you because of the rain. It's the rain that allows me to offer to give you notes on your film, if you want."

Delivered in lowered tones, my entire story is bullshit. While I speak, the barista retrieves some tea and a small Chihuahua from behind the coffee bar, and when I am done, she informs me that the cold brew has been made, and we are free to converse for the moment at hand. While I was speaking, her avoidance of looking anywhere near me made me think she was irritated, and that maybe I was exhibiting an internalized toxic masculinity by wanting someone to listen to me while I talked and talked, all because I had been ghosted and insulted by a woman who I thought cared about me. But the thing was, I didn't care that I was behaving like a problematic male. I let the anger grow, tightening the muscles in my upper and central back.

The girl's eyes dart about as she speaks. "This is my service dog, Jam the Good Chihuahua. It was between Jam and

Yam, because jam is always good whereas yams, uh, well, it depends on how you make them. Everyone knows that dogs, generally, are always good not bad, except for certain stereotyped breeds, one of which is the Chihuahua. So, in protest of expectation, I went with Jam and not Yam."

She is talking borderline nonsense. In my own story, I digressed and made rabbit trails because I thought she would, and I was right. She lacks focus. Her dog regards me with pecan-colored eyes and a camel hair coat fastened over fur of the same color.

The boy shuffles to the restroom. I note the ensconcing of the perimeter with white paper bags, placed along the back ledges of the wooden booths that abut the curtain wall. The white paper bags have the air of hiding plastic tea candles, unlit.

"My tented luminescence," explains the barista. "Would you perchance star in my short film? I'd need you as 'casual bystander.' You'd need to drink coffee, but if you can't, because you're jittery already, I could give you decaf, but, and don't take this the wrong way, I really wouldn't want you to drink water, even though you could, and not tea either, because I'm really all about authenticity, and not in the way it sounds, but like, really."

"Lovely. Tell me more." But I'm exhausted, and—were it acceptable to do so—would spread out right there on the floor.

She keeps talking: "Oh, and I forgot to mention. So this will be for my class, Film and Contemporary Dance. When you film dance, you want to get it from every angle, and so I film the dancers over and over from every position until I can cut from angle to angle while representing continuous movement, like in 'Nine Variations on a Dance Theme' by Hilary Harris. Have you seen it?"

"I know the piece," I say, and think of my Lea in my dream, her palm descending along my torso.

"Well," she goes on, seemingly about to talk forever, "I'm not doing *such* a close-up in any of my shots as Harris, but I am doing the repetition litany. I'll do it with three dancers instead of one. I want to show the layering of worlds. The heavenly Jupiter, Neptune's watery world, and the dark rendition by Pluto. I have them in different leotards, yellow, blue, and black to symbolize the gods, and I chose them for their respective light, ruminative, and brooding styles. And you know that point when the film goes chaotic with the discordant chords?"

I nod. It's a blank, curt, stingy nod. My face lacks expression. She can't take a hint.

"That's when I'm thinking I'll switch the dancers to different locations within the coffee shop, their bodies will still be at the same angles in relation to the position of the camera, but…"

At this point, I am not listening. I am thinking of my bad emotion, how it is still an emotion, and what I will do with my sadness at the rejection of my Lea. I've already moved past a toxic moment, and I'm ready to leave and go process. But this girl is saying something about the bar and how her eating disorder caused her to fixate on it. I can't make sense of what she is saying, moving from snacks to alcohol to cancer, but she rubs her dog's head and thanks me effusively, bouncing in her clogs.

"Talking to you made me realize I need to put her at the bar table! Ah, brilliant."

"I can't take any credit for that idea, I am just the wall to which you reflected, the paper to your pen, so to speak, but my advice would be to make your concept more direct and physical and less associative. You need more embodiment. Otherwise, Jupiter's, Neptune's, and Pluto's identities won't come through. Unless you film in mists, or aether, quintessence, the fifth element, you know? Or perhaps in water, beside a creek, say, for Neptune, and Pluto maybe beside a fire, probably at night."

"Oh, dear. I feel so ignorant talking to you! You must really be an incredible proffy. Do you like that term, 'proffy'? It's almost like the word 'babe' or 'baby.' It can be so basic, but I like it ironically anyway." She speaks more absently now, looking out the windows, and scratches her dog's back under the camel hair coat. "I'll probably add a misty scene, too, just to see if I like how it looks? I mean, I don't know if I'll really take your advice, no offense, but I'm still *so grateful* because talking to you made me realize, just, so many things. So, thanks."

This is what I do, nudge realizations of the next obvious step, break things down. I have nothing left to say, and I do not even manage a smile. But it's no matter, because the barista leaves me with the justification of a new customer at the bell-jangling door. What do I do with myself now? Classes are not yet started. I have nothing to do but work on my syllabus.

I sit down, my bones feeling almost rusted, pained, and I compose a grocery list.

> black ppr
> onions
> coffee
> tide pods
> a brain
> fresh flowers
> the burnt smell of regret, like dead fish
> the thing i'll run out of, which i've forgotten

The rain has finally let up, so I head out even though my moccasins will get wet. I think of a friend from middle school and her pantry full of junk food. Strange, how she had portraits of her bodybuilder parents, who owned a gym, and yet the pantry was filled with those sweets. Oatmeal cream pies, brown sugar Pop-Tarts, waxy brownies in the shapes of Christmas trees with fat sprinkles for ornaments. I used to lose control there, like Lea is doing right now with some man.

I walk home and count numbers of gray things. Under a charcoal roof, the eighth gray object, stacks of comic books wilt and sag on a puddled porch. At the intersection, my Lea appears. We approach one another, and she nods at something behind me. "There goes my date," she calls, too loud.

I guess she has the need to insult him. I turn to see the receding figure of a tall, thin man with long hair.

"He was fine. How was your day, babe?"

I give her my last letter, which details my dream, the one she hasn't heard. "I'm jealous."

"Of me, dating? You could be dating, too." She flicks her bangs out of her eyes and regards the letter. "I'll read later, okay? Wanna go to the movies? We can sneak in candy…"

I stop and look at my shoes. "The rain," I say. "I want to change."

"Jesus. You really can't take care of yourself, can you?"

"Wet moccasins. It's an old name."

She turns toward her car, still at the café, and I follow toward the tea candles, which I can see are on. Jupiter is dancing on the bar, dressed head to toe in gold.

WETS'A
𐓷𐓘́𐓤'𐓘

The spiders of Los Angeles wove their webs, succulents dripped with dew, and jealousy struck my heart while leaving the Wazhazhe moccasin-making meetup at Laurel and Hardy Park.

think I fucked my phone up babe it fell in water fuck

The text from B stopped me still in front of the old Osage ladies, who glanced at me in concern. My sun umbrella tipped out of my tote and we saw that the sun had edged my shoulders from medium beige to deep brown. I^shdaxi^ waleze—*tan lines*—could get me fired from the runway show that night. I shoved my supplies and phone into my bag and headed off.

"Kashikada^ iwithe dv mi^kshe!" I called, using the full formulation of the phrase meaning I'd see them again. I felt that it was colonized and dangerous to use anglicized abbreviations in our speech, but all the same they called back, "Iwithe!" I tried to smile.

"Wait," one called, and offered me a bundle of flowers from her purse. "Wets'aoitse eko^," she said.

I received the yellow bouquet. "Rattlesnake-like?" I translated. "I don't know much about plants."

"Yes, exactly. It's yarrow. It promotes regeneration, like a snake shedding its skin." Her kind, wrinkled eyes were beautiful, and she had a cold that made her Wazhazhe ie nasalizations sound smooth and skillful. I was unsure how to feel but I thanked her anyway, for making our day together good.

The women's chatter receded as I cut up an alley, then turned right on another, toward the corner of Sunset and Parkman, where I took the phone out to reread the text. The eyes of the ancestor saved on my lock screen met mine. A great-great-grandfather, he was half-European, half-Native, like B. Unlike B, the ancestor was known for his ability to talk to snakes. He had introduced himself to me in a dream after I hooked up with this girl who had a snake tattoo sleeve beginning on her left leg and extending up her body. Not long after, B and I met on a daylong layover in Denver. I had first spotted him taking a selfie under a mural titled *In the Middle of Now/here*.

I started texting him back but got distracted rereading our last exchange.

Hey babe, going to sleep, love you

think I fucked my phone up babe it fell in water fuck

[...]

[...]

[...]

I typed with the bunch of yarrow tucked under my arm, but kept erasing every message. It had taken him sixteen hours to text me back since he'd been away in Palm Springs at a bachelor party, and while I was relieved that he was okay, I couldn't help but worry that he was fucking up more than his phone. But he was not a bad guy. I tried to think positively, and decided not to text. As I approached my favorite coffee shop, my thoughts turned to Ines of the snake tattoo. A text from her had also come back in the park, and I had been waiting to open it. It was the first I'd heard from her since we hooked up in Big Bear during a hike in the woods. I tapped on the message to find a seminude, in which her sliver of ass had grown into curves, so that she was now S-shaped from her chest to her hips like the Quetzalcoatl encircling her waist. I gaped at the photo and almost walked into a street sign. Sunset Boulevard. How many times had I walked this street at night, drunk, with boys, some of whom I sent nudes to? And now, I was sober, heading home, not sending but receiving.

I examined the photo not as a sexual beneficiary, but as a former creator and co-conspirator. Ines's hip was popped, and her jutting shoulder framed the snake's tongue hanging out at me, ready to bathe me in flames. Her areolas were the size of dandelions. It was too overwhelming, so I put my phone away and focused on my breath in counts of six until I reached the order window. I asked for an Americano, straight, no sugar, which I couldn't consume, along with dairy, soy, white wheat, peanuts, canola oil. Colonial foods made me break out, and because I'd once had to mitigate the acne with birth control pills, I had the double outcome of clear skin and childlessness.

Before I could even get my coffee, Ines followed up with another photo. In this one, she'd put on her rainbow-hued Wu-Tang Clan shirt and was sticking out her tongue with her eyes closed and her nose scrunched up. Her curly hair fanned out around her head. Recent dye stained the skin under her ear. I hearted it and asked the barista for a vegan muffin. His black nail polish reminded me of the grabbing fingers of Beverly Hills women on vacation in Palm Springs. I thanked him and leaned against the wall of the building. The day was hot and windy and the muffin was moist and of the darkest, bitterest chocolate. The taste gave me great pleasure, and my cheeks ached as Ines's shape drifted into my memory. Her brittle frame had preoccupied me during sex on the mountain hike, because I knew what it was like to be that close to disappearing. As we reached inside one another on that rock in Big Bear, there seemed to be a mutual attempt between us to transcend breakability, to cherish and seduce ourselves into a safer kind of living.

As I threw the muffin wrapper away, I felt a strange sense of my own realness, and of Ines's. Tears came to my eyes. I left with my espresso and headed east. My body was filling with a sudden panic, and I couldn't drink more than a few sips before I gave the coffee to a homeless woman. Her eyes were covered in heavy eyeliner, and as we glanced at one another, I realized why Ines had sent me the pictures.

She wanted me to show them to B.

I tapped some thoughts into my phone:

1. Ines really wants the threesome. Considering it for her, because if I do it with B in mind I am afraid that I would end up leaving him and I am not ready
2. Love him the middle amount, not enough for sacrifice or casual enough for carefree
3. A little bit in love with Ines and we are both trying to transform our womanhood
4. I feel there isn't any way for me to say no to either of them

I let my anger toward B grow. Why had he never shared his location with me? I was sharing mine with him, even now. And why had I not asked him to? Asking him for anything seemed impossible. It was as though we were sitting at opposite ends of a very long negotiating table, and the places we were starting from seemed too disparate for meeting in the middle. He was pushing for a threesome, arguing it had to be with one of my friends and not a stranger, and claiming that the intimate communication necessary to pull it off would make us stronger and help me *explore* my sexuality, whereas I just wanted shelter. I did what I had to in order to get it.

I reached the apartment, set the yarrow on the table, and stripped down in front of the bathroom mirror to check my tan lines. My shoulders, arms, and legs were darker than my stomach and chest, but the difference wasn't as bad as I'd thought it would be. There was enough time to do the laundry so B wouldn't get mad, so I put on a house robe and took a load down the rickety, paint-peeling steps into the basement laundry room we shared with the other units. Wathila^ ashkape, *he gets mad easy*, and though girlfriends joked about the dependency of Native men, he had never been violent like the non-Native guy I dated before him. I felt safest here, of anywhere I'd been, and I justified my labor by claiming him as my protector, reminding myself that I'd already changed him from outright yelling to sulking by almost leaving, and it was possible that he would change more.

I double-checked the pockets for tissues while a blond in face-framing curls came in and set himself up at the machine two down from me. He had his girlfriend's or boyfriend's laundry, lacy panties and lounge wear. It was unthinkable to me that a man would do *a female's* laundry.

"I like your nails," he said.

"Oh, thanks," I said.

"Self-care is so important," he said, apparently referring to his washing. Maybe the panties were his, or I was misgendering. The person's nails were naked and smooth.

"Do you ever like to get your nails done?" I asked.

"I'm just water, vitamin D, therapy, and I do like to do one thing for myself every week. Just for me. So, yeah, I've had a pedicure, yeah. And community is important. I love my radical activist community."

I suppressed a smile. Was he saying this because he thought it would impress me? My reds were almost ready to go. This guy reminded me of a profile of a radical Black farmer I'd read a zinester interview with, in which he'd said that the process of staying alive had led him to work out, drink water, get sun, and go to therapy as a baseline of self-care. B could benefit from some of this stuff, I thought, resolving to share the profile and laundry room story with him. I opened a washer and the guy happened to glance over in time to see as a garter snake coiled around the plastic agitator, looking up at us with what seemed like an expression of reticence.

"Jesus Christ!" he said.

I held my laundry over the curling animal. Ines said snakes mean *power.*

The blond's eyes questioned my calm face. "That's crazy," he said.

While I was curious what his activist community was, I didn't have the energy to stay here, with him, and the snake.

"Forget it," I said with a wave, "I'll do this later. Take care."

He also was hot, which was irritating. In the past, I might have pursued him. He made me think of Oklahoma, when I was seeing a designer, my California boyfriend, and a Maya Ch'ortí girl who'd picked me up at Kihekah Steh Powwow. She connected me with the modeling agency in Los Angeles, as is the way of polyamory—sex becomes a network, ever unknowing of what new lovers will embody, where they will lead us, or when we'll grow apart or be left behind.

I put on a cold shower to help with the tan lines, my brain on overdrive. The designer would be there, and I needed to review. At our last date, we'd had dinner at his place, and he'd asked about my relationship history. He deemed my prior relationship abusive and told me I needed to heal. Without so much as a touch or kiss, he gave me other advice, ending with the scenario that, all things settled, we would marry. In response, I put my coat on and left, confident any relationship with him would be problematic, if not abusive. At least he hired me.

I toweled off and dressed, mulling the question of whether I *should* have broken up with B, as the designer had urged. I couldn't decide, but this idea of a choice was possibly also an illusion. The point of the snake was that I needed to be on *my own* side, but this advice struck me as isolating, inconvenient, and even impossible. I continued thinking these things around in circles, and forgot to write B a note reminding him about the show as I left, with one last glance at the yarrow propped in the sink. On a whim, I put it in my bag.

In the car, I tried calling him, forgetting about his dead phone for a moment. He needed to rely on me less anyway. I was at least half the reason for his dependence on me. If he didn't have me, maybe he would have become like these self-care men of women's magazines and my laundry room, seeking out their own therapy.

The interminable light at my last turn had me inching and I could barely believe that this was my first runway show in the city. I'd walked at Indian Market in Santa Fe, but it was different here. This was a private show in preparation for Fashion Week, and the designs would be worn for the first time after all the fittings. I turned on the song with the bpm I had practiced my spins to, and visualized posture and steps in my mind as I arrived at an old theater-turned-club.

I walked from my parking spot, through the back service doors, and into a throng of people. A makeup artist quickly ushered me into a chair and my phone buzzed with texts as I apologized for being late. "I must've got the wrong memo," I said.

"You're fine." In her drawl, I recognized the Oklahoma version of the saying, a slightly defensive but affirming statement that we were in a place of mutual respect. That made me feel at home, and I settled in and focused on relaxing my shoulders. The last thing I needed was a stiff runway walk.

My phone was still unlocked, and I glanced quickly at what Ines was saying:

If daddy isn't down for the threesome, we could find our own man!!

Ever since she had kissed me, I'd stopped feeling like I could confide in her. The only reason I had tolerated the mention of a threesome anyway, long ago, was to avoid commitment. Now I was more locked in than ever and increasingly all I was wanting was to be free. The phone was dying, and still no text from B, whose phone "fell in water." It sounded like a lie and even if it wasn't, he was the type of careful person who didn't drop anything, unless too drunk. Still, I did not have and couldn't afford my own apartment. I was not in a place to be wanting threesomes; what I wanted was shelter. If B wanted careless sex, enabling, and on top of this, to get drunk and ignore me, I could choose to leave him, but the question was where would *I stay*? Ines was the only person I could think of, and now she demanded sexual compliance, too.

"Look up," said the artist. She was pretty, with a round face like mine, brown-skinned but not tanned. Her face was properly roundish where mine was more oval.

"Where are you from?" she asked.

"A small town in northeast Oklahoma," I murmured, trying to keep my jaw from moving.

"You can talk," she said, softening. "I do the lips last. Just *keep still.*"

She asked me what it was like, my small northeast Oklahoma town.

"Well, I lived in an apartment complex in our little downtown area, which is growing, because a TV food star has a restaurant there. It's called The Rancher's Home. Have you heard of it? She lives illegally on our land that some of her ancestors stole. Still, she gives jobs and coffee to the Indians in town, and her coffee's good as the stuff we have around here. I fit in there, but I wanted a man. I am trying to see if I can fit in here."

She put her brush in the green lip paint we were wearing. "Are you Native? I know the designer for this show is."

"That's how I got this job. He did some work on my rez once."

I opened my language app to show her. "Ahai," I read, and showed her our orthography. "This is our language."

"That looks like some alien shit!" she said.

"It is. A saying goes, 'We are stars.'"

I wanted to ask her if she was connected to any other nations, but before I could she sent me off to the gray area rug where the designer stood with the others. He came right up to me and I felt wordless and suddenly not there at all. I started thinking of groceries, of all things. I needed to—had forgotten to—get groceries. In front of me were the brown boots of the designer, and he was talking. The boots were the same as the ones B had worn out the door to the bachelor party. I had to cover my mouth and act like I was yawning because I couldn't breathe.

"Are you ready?" he said.

I looked up at his eyes. They were kind, and tired.

"Follow me," he said. All the models moved. We went behind the stage area and he unveiled twelve terrariums, each home to a yellow snake.

"Isla, please step forward."

One of the snakes was looking at me. I shook my head at the animal. *Not again,* I imagined myself speaking to it in ESP. *I reject your washing machine advice and you insist on coming back to me now?*

The snake stuck its tongue out.

"I am always *down* for everything," the designer went on, "because I am from the desert."

Thurston Moore's "Ono Soul" was playing from the speakers. The bass and drums hit and the designer's voice dropped. "So you will all be walking with snakes. Isla?" he said again.

The snake would cover the lines of my tan, and it was not a particular taboo in my own tribal background, but I was worried I should do more research. For instance, B's tribe was totally anti-snake. The girl beside me grabbed my hand. We were all Native, and I had met this girl at an Ojibwe designer's show. This designer, like other Native designers, was known for walking with lineups of Indigenous models, but this snake scene was too much.

Candace stepped forward. "Isla might be okay with this, and I know you're Laguna, but I'm Diné and personally I am not okay with this. I believe that it's culturally insensitive."

The designer nodded, but he was still looking at me. I stepped forward. "There was a snake in my washing machine earlier today. I'm happy to go first or last so not all the models have to do this."

"I can't walk in this show," said Candace. "You should have told us."

This broke the still air. Everlee, who was shaking, went to the snakes. I demonstrated a smooth walk. Shoulders back, head level, face grateful but not excited. Feet in one single line, pace even, feet steady, body fluid and supple, I spun slowly, and the snake slid on my shoulder.

"No one who doesn't want to walk with a snake will have to. If you have to go home…"

Candace was staring at her own feet. I felt bad for her.

The designer was being inconsiderate, but I still couldn't help but admire him for getting his work into a Fashion Week show, even if it was in L.A. and not New York. I knew I shouldn't think that way, because he was being problematic, but I was sick of people never thinking of Natives on our own land. He removed the snake from my shoulders, and we all dressed in the sheer and sandy-colored browns and reds that wrapped around our bodies like Laguna-style leggings. My dress was overlaid with glittery cut-glass beads, and he placed the snake on me.

I felt my ancestors on my shoulder blades and imagined the painting hanging on my wall at home, the one with the *x*'s and *I*'s representing the generations before me:

x

I

xx

II

xxxx

IIII

xxxxxxxx

IIIIII

xxxxxxxxxxxxxxxx

IIIIIIIIIIIIIIII

xxxxxxxxxxxxxxxxxxxxxxxxxxxxxxxx

IIIIIIIIIIIIIIIIIIIIIIIIIIIIIIII

xxxxxxxxxxxxxxxxxxxxxxxxxxxxxxxxxxxxxxxxxxxxxxxxxxxxxxxxxxxxxxxx

I went forward, under the snake, into the line, and onto the runway.

My balance was strong and I hit every turn, and I also felt connected with the audience, who struck me as people like me, everyday heartbroken players of life. As soon as the handler took the snake from my shoulders and I got back to drink some water, I heard my name yelled in muffled tones of panic.

It was B, trying to get in through the service doors.

He must have come back, followed my location, and now he was losing it, flying into a rage. I had seen this happen to him before, when once or twice, early in our relationship, he'd given in to delusions of jealousy. In the past, I would've tried to help him, but my hand was not moving from its locked grip on the service door handle.

I remembered a dream I'd had the night before, of an old-time Native woman in a small modern-day cabin with red bruises on her neck. She had told me to become two-spirit. It was a strange dream, and I had pushed it away, but now it seemed clear. Maybe the yarrow was helping. It was sitting in my model bag, and I thought I could smell it, though it was several feet away from me. With the inhalation, I saw what would happen if I opened the door.

"*What are you* doing *here?!*" he was screaming.

I moved backward.

If he was violent, my face could be damaged to a point that it would threaten my job prospects. I knew part of him was trying to protect me, and maybe he thought I was here against my will, but I didn't trust him in his confusion. My intuition told me not to open the door. I reminded myself how I'd felt these past twenty-four hours. I looked at his last text, then I stopped sharing my location with him, and I got my bag.

My movements felt robotic, my body numb as I exited through the front door. Candace was putting her own bag in her car and I walked over to her, breathing deeply and hoping it would soften the shaking in my hands.

"What's wrong?"

"I need to get away," I said. "No time to explain."

"Skoden," she said.

Instead of yelling that phrase joyfully, in its common usage, she almost whispered. We both heard B out back, crying and yelling, still banging on the door. I also heard the designer's voice, then a bouncer's. They would call the police, I thought, and began to run back, but Candace grabbed me. "He won't call them," she said. She thought the same way as I did.

I doubled over crying and my phone fell out of the designer's dress pocket.

"Someone's calling you," said Candace. She read the name of one of the older Osage women from my meet-up.

"It's my friend Edith," I said. "Answer it."

She put it on speaker. "Hello, I'm Isla's friend. I'm here with her. Something's happened—I think she's in shock."

"Oh, okay."

"We're in a crisis," Candace added.

"Okay," she said, apparently unbothered. "I was calling to ask if she knew anyone who might be able to use yarrow, because I have so much. But never mind that. What's going on?"

I spoke up finally. "Hi, it's me. I can't go home."

There was almost no pause at all. "Why don't you come over here?"

"That would be very helpful," I said. Candace took down Edith's address while I put my bag in the back seat and buckled up. I wanted to fall apart further, and to go to B, but I managed to wait out that feeling with another bout of weeping. I was so worried that he would die if they called the police, or simply that he would get in trouble, and it would affect his career. I wanted so badly to go to him, but I knew that doing so would only make things worse.

"I think I might need to stay there tonight," I said, choking the words out.

Candace held my hand and teared up. "I think that's a great idea," she said.

"You bet you're staying here," said Edith. Candace started to drive and I thought how grateful I was to have friends. I let myself be moved by her extraordinarily shiny hair in the passing streetlights. It calmed me. By the time we got to Edith's small home of cedar shakes half covered in azalea bushes, we were hungry. The old woman gave us pot roast. Her cold had improved, and her voice was clear with a gentle timbre. I told her she sounded different, and she said she'd had yarrow tea. She made me some tea, too, and I went to bed and thought again of my ancestor painting, but imagined it doubling in a mirror pattern, traveling backward and forward at once.

x

I

xx

II

xxxx

IIII

xxxxxxxx

IIIIIII

xxxxxxxxxxxxxxxx

IIIIIIIIIIIIII

xxxxxxxxxxxxxxxxxxxxxxxxxxxxxxxx

IIIIIIIIIIIIIIIIIIIIIIIIIIII

xxxxxxxxxxxxxxxxxxxxxxxxxxxxxxxxxxxxxxxxxxxxxxxxxxxxxxxxxxxxxxxx

IIIIIIIIIIIIIIIIIIIIIIIIIIII

xxxxxxxxxxxxxxxxxxxxxxxxxxxxxxxx

IIIIIIIIIIIIII

xxxxxxxxxxxxxxxx

IIIIIII

xxxxxxxx

IIII

xxxx

xx

I

X

MY KIND OF WOMAN

Ride the wild winds
for dangerous knowledge.

All night.

—Joy Harjo, "Exile of Memory"

Once you stop caring about anything, it's hard to begin again. Your body has turned off all concern, without the consent of your conscious mind, without even the use of drugs. The eyes feel vacant. You become one who is not, as the saying goes, all there. The year I met Rose, I was living like this. My family had not heard from me in years, and on Christmas night, Rose and I bonded over a bottle of wine in the lobby of a Flagstaff hotel.

It was really vodka, but we called it wine in our text messages to each other. Why? It is the level of denial necessary to make a game of your own life: you must first lie to yourself. That was our general habit. We finished the bottle just before sunrise, napped, walked around the mall, saw a movie, and then I slept some more. When I woke, Rose was gone. I did not think I would hear from her again.

She was a famous singer. I don't know her real name, but her stage name was Rosella, though most who knew her called her Rose. I was an unknown musician living in a remote Oklahoma tribal reservation. We met by chance, at a funeral, when a mutual friend introduced us. He was Cherokee, my tenth-grade crush and Rose's college hallmate. We stood over a bowl of fruit punch and he noted quietly that we both wore gray dresses in a room filled with black and blue. Soon the boy, and his observations, receded, as Rose and I agreed that we had both lost many others in the same way as the person we were mourning. Lost all from drugs or hard living, less from fault of their own than from how difficult it was to live in this world as anything *othered*.

We exchanged numbers and texted sometimes over the following months, about nothing. We sent each other obscure music videos, and when we later found ourselves on the road in the Southwest during the holidays, avoiding family, we met up to drink. She told me she had a boyfriend in Pawhuska, a six-foot-four redhead who liked her ten pounds heavy, or "Oklahoma perfect" as he liked to say. I stared at the icy blue eyes in the picture she showed me, and confessed, without boasting, that I was a teacher and had never had a real boyfriend. I wondered why she had a boyfriend like that, but I figured she found that region interesting and was writing an album touching on Oklahoma. I hoped that our friendship lasted longer than the boyfriend.

Months later, in the beginning of spring, my single "Washka^" topped a major music blog's best singles of the year list and Rose, apparently partial to her new friend, reached out. She wanted me to come out to L.A. to cowrite some songs. I was in Pawhuska, emotionally hungover, and indecisive after a year working on an album in Wazhazhe ie. Still, I drove out, stopping in Santa Fe at a friend's who always put me up. Late Sunday, I made it to Rose's house on Mulholland Drive.

Rosella lived in a Spanish revival of light pink stucco with a tile roof, and her front door was unlocked. I entered a mint-green foyer filled with palmettos and a tan carpet that spread to a white baby grand piano with an open lid. The Yamaha sat in the front of a long room papered in vertical stripes like French silk ribbons. Rosella was at the far end, pale and tucked into a brown leather couch, sipping coffee. She had the air of a small woman trapped in a canyon echoing with the last vibrations of her rage. She struck me as exhausted but peaceful; dead in her expression but living in her beauty, the heat of her cheeks going pink and accentuating the clear, bright whites of her eyes.

"The front door was open," I said, out of a sudden fear she would take offense to my entry.

"Not at all, please sit." I did as she said. We were both the type to be out of it—floating above—but we tried to pay attention to one another. "Well. I'm so glad you came," she added. "Would you like something to drink?"

"I'm jonesing for a pop."

"Soda pop?" she says. "Mm-hmm." She went to the kitchen and came back with a can of Diet Dr Pepper for me. "Is this okay?"

I opened the can in answer while she went and made herself espresso by pushing a button on a little glossy red machine by her record player. The room was beautiful, and I took it in. Framed giant poppies lined the ribbon walls.

"Are these real?" I indicated the flowers with my index finger, its nail painted blue.

"They were grown in a lab and pressed in a huge book. I just liked them."

Small talk over, she tossed a silk housecoat behind her and bent to examine a bookshelf full of records. I noticed a lime-green record on the player, skipping at the end of its side. I went over, picked the needle up, and dropped it on the first concentric rings, but the volume was too low and I could not hear the song.

Rose stood abruptly and looked me over. I was wearing torn-up shorts, two sizes too big, with bleach spots in a homemade attempt at ombré. Deciding against another record selection, she instead went back to her couch and opened a voice memo she had requested from me. I had recorded it in the car on the drive over, and titled the file "sunset song." I turned the record player off, and we both listened to my singing voice, pained and clear-noted but too loud.

> *Between Needles and L.A. / I was eight hours away / coming Californ-i-a for the second time that way / with everything I own in the back of my car to fornicate at the end of the stars / it felt illegal baby to move in on ya driving Ninety-Five into orange sky but in the end / I just couldn't believe I wasn't worth every sunset all the blue and pink / I gave up molly got off apple pie model nine-to-five then bead and talk—*

At the piano Rose played a triad in G. I felt a dopamine rush at the sight of her furry, clear plastic high-heeled shoes clicking on the damper pedal. She circled through leading chords, I, IV, V.

I sang some more:

> *What the hell am I supposed to do / when I don't want to be in love with you / stop rubbing your face on mine up in the bar / if you don't wanna love me for the rest of your li-i-i-ife!*

Rose stopped playing and asked me what I was thinking about.

"A guy in my band," I said. "He came on to me when I thought it was safe to be friends. He used to drink whiskey from a mug that said 'Give a damn!' at the studio."

Her long nails clicked on the black keys.

Finally, she closed the piano. "Do you like Walmart?"

I laughed. "After you left Flagstaff, I went to Walmart. Bought leggings. It was cold out."

"I'm sure it's big in Pawhuska," she observed.

"Walmart is forty minutes away from Pawhuska. Sometimes I walk around there to be alone. I've spent hours walking around, dreaming about people becoming who they want to be through acquiring stuff. Competent Housewife with plates and teakettles. Seamstress shopping fabrics. Marathon Runner in need of muscle rollers and protein bars. Do you need something from there? I can go for you, if you ever need, so you're not mauled. It's a cultural experience."

As soon as I offered, I felt the comment was idiotic. I'd been unable to restrain myself.

"No," she said. "I'm not that famous." But it wasn't true. She was. It was ludicrous that I was here. In that moment, I didn't even understand or remember how it had happened. "Never mind," she said. "Do you wanna go to the beach? We can have Slushees. And finish writing in Malibu. We might see the dolphins. It's that time. And then we can go for dinner at this cute diner in Topanga."

I remember thinking that there must be a fancy 7-Eleven in Malibu. The notion made me laugh aloud. I imagined Rose driving in reverse down her steep, palm-lined driveway.

"Definitely," I said. "I'd be down."

"I want to take a nap first. Go in a few hours? You can make yourself at home."

I said sure and sank onto some cushions on the floor, criss-cross applesauce, the way my kindergarteners sit at circle time.

"Othoda," I tell them all. "What does that mean?"

"Behave!" they say in chorus.

Rose spread out on the couch and immediately went to sleep. After a while, I stopped looking at all the stuff in the room and went through sliding glass doors to a backyard patio. There was a pool, though not guitar-shaped like I had imagined. I slipped in wearing my white T-shirt and jean shorts and the fabrics soaked through and pulled on my body, relaxing me. Rose did not come out, and I got out of the pool, with all the excess water in my clothes rushing down my body like tiny rapids. I stood there, waiting to dry, creating this small drama as an excuse to meditate for a couple of minutes, so that by the time I was no longer actively dripping, I felt ready to continue with Rose on our song. I peeked in to check on her, but she was still motionless on the couch, as if the coffee she had made herself had contained a tranquilizer. I shed my clothes and spread them on the hot stone patio to dry, then spent an hour drifting between the jet tub and the pool, until I finally grew tired and left her a note on a grocery receipt from my pocket.

It was water-printed and blurry with slanted handwriting.

> *I like your wing-tipped orange eyeshadow. I'm going to go try to find some and get another pop bc I'm still thirsty. And I just wanted to ask you, do you think if you felt better, it would mean you would stop being an artist, and what would you do?*

I threw my plastic pen down and ran out the back gate, ripping one rose head off the bush. A thorn tore the skin of my thumb, and I seemed to bleed pink. There, in the shade, I decided I didn't want to come back to this place. It hit me that there was no reason for me to be here. I wasn't on her level. She wanted a "reservation" cowrite, or else, if she really did believe in me, I was just too freaked out and felt jilted by her weird avoidant napping.

On the drive home, I listened to all her albums in a row. It was sunset when I went through the green lights in Needles, and by the time I got to the Joshua trees near the Hualapai I was overcome with tiredness. It was cooling off in the desert, so I pulled over and slept. I didn't have the capacity to think about it or worry, but I was lucky no one bothered me. In Flagstaff, I gassed up and got coffee and continued toward my friend's open door in Santa Fe. Then, still hours away, I remembered that Rose had said something once about the El Rancho Hotel in Gallup, so I pulled off and slipped into the bar there. I had a couple of margaritas and went outside to smoke with the security guy, who said there was an unbooked room and I could sleep there if I didn't mind ghosts.

"My place where I live is actually haunted. It's because a lot of people were murdered there, even my own great-grandmother," I said.

"Dang. I'm very sorry to hear that." The guy I was talking to was skinny and brown and he looked like he wanted a cigarette so I offered.

He accepted. "Where is home for you, generally speaking?"

"On my rez in Oklahoma. Before we were on that land, we were in Kansas, and the settlers there were shooting us, just anytime, for no reason, or I guess more like any tiny reason they could invent, such as if we killed a deer. As in, they'd put up signs that read 'no deer killing' and then if we killed one to eat it they'd kill us; or even just for sport, some of them, they would kill us. There were bands of white people called Injun Killers who wore fringe, and we were losing so many, we were being pushed out of there. The Cherokees had some land we were looking at buying, so we sent a person out there in the form of a wolf. The scout took the form of the wolf and checked out the land, and they said that it had black stuff under the ground and that it would make us rich."

"Dang," he said. It was all he could say. "I'm from East L.A."

"I was just there," I said, and I told him I'd take him up on the room but that I couldn't hang out at all anymore. "I'm getting really tired," I told him.

"Yeah, nah, it's not like that—"

We finished our cigarettes and I followed him into the lobby. For some reason, I felt the need to explain: "The reason I'm good with ghosts is because they've always been around my whole life, and I'm good at kind of ignoring them, or living around them, or whatever."

"Cool, cool. I know what you mean."

He gave me the key and showed me to the room, which was on the first floor by a timeline of the Navajo Nation, and though I could've worried that he had *another* key and since he had given me this room free there would be some kind of *price,* I just didn't have the space in my brain to care. I lay down on the bed and crashed out, just like that. I woke up at 10 a.m. and while I was splashing water on my face and heading out of there, it occurred to me that I had so much luck. What if I could get out of my lease and go live in L.A. with Rose for a bit?

The next morning, back in Pawhuska, I went to see my landlord in her gift shop.

My landlord had a face like a figurine's, with a small curved nose and large unmoving lips. I couldn't bring myself to say anything at first, I was too tired. She was both serene and hardened in her mask of a quiet face.

I pointed at my T-shirt for the tribal school. "I'm going to quit. It's time to move on."

My landlord smiled, which shocked me. Dark brown freckles spread like a Band-Aid on her nose. "Good for you. It seems like it might be about time."

"Really? That's great. I'll take this candle," I said gratefully, moving a soy candle sprinkled with lavender toward her and pulling out my wallet.

"All right," she said with an approving nod. I felt blessed.

I went back up to get ready for work and turned the burner on to heat water for coffee. When I was almost done with my makeup, I started to smell smoke. I ran into the kitchen to find a three-foot-tall grease fire. I'd turned on the wrong burner, and the pan I'd used to fry eggs the night before had lit up. There was a tiny fire extinguisher on the wall, and I used it to put out the flames. I cleaned, and then emailed my two weeks' notice to my boss, the principal of the school, and texted my landlord to confirm I was leaving.

When I got in to work, the principal told me not to bother. "Just go," she said.

So I did. I went home and continued cleaning things up for a few hours; then I moved all my possessions into my car and called up a musician friend who lived in Broken Arrow. We met up at an arcade and played *Pac-Man*, and when I told her about writing with Rosella and how I'd decided to quit teaching, she said she supported the whole endeavor and I could crash with her. When we got to her place, there was a guy with roached hair whose name was Jess. He called my friend "Shells," which seemed over-familiar to me. Then he went back to watching a movie that was showing a screaming woman with her T-shirt ripped open. I didn't know what it was, and I didn't care. Jess was Shelli's coworker at a restaurant where they were both line cooks, and he waved as I went to Shelli's room. Soon, both were gone to work, and I was alone.

The principal called my phone then, but I declined the call and blocked her. She was known to yell out of turn, and I didn't need that.

A text followed, from my landlord.

This is not a slum.

Had I not been clear enough in our conversation at her shop? I racked my memory, trying to think if I'd left any stuff in there, but I could only remember a mop and bucket in the pantry.

"I told you. Did you not get my text…" I started, but she called me.

"I said *this is not a slum.*"

I was beginning to think she had me confused with someone else. I had heard her use that phrase before, when people moved out and dumped old beds in the hallway, or when they left their last socks and cords and hairdryers and dirty linens—the last ten percent of belongings—abandoned and the place not yet clean. She was claiming I was one of them—she was calling me trash.

She hung up on me.

I called her back, but it went straight to voice mail. "Shit," I said.

A small dog wandered in from another room and we stared at each other.

"What?" I said.

I called my landlord again, but no luck. I made myself a bowl of hominy soup and ate a bar made out of dried fruit. I watched more of the television show, in which the woman was now carrying bottles of nail polish around and crying. I didn't understand. I began to worry I had made a mistake with my plans to leave, that I was abandoning myself, and I decided to attend a Wazhazhe cultural event the next day. It was a meat-pie-making language activity. I thought about our language, and how we had to constantly show to the federal government that we had a language, without revitalizing it so strongly that they would think we were a threat. Or at least I assumed that was the reason we refused to do the total immersion strategy. That night, I read about a Gaelic man who visited North American tribes and led them through a language revitalization program that had worked in Scotland. I decided to ask my language teacher about it at the event, but I would not get to see her. Instead, when I stepped out of my overstuffed car in the grass parking lot outside of Wakon Iron Community Hall, a cop was there.

He drew his weapon: "Hands up."

I put them up. Then he informed me I was under arrest for breaking my lease, deserting a premises, and failure to pay damages.

"But we're in Indian Camp."

"Do you have intent to resist?"

"No, but I thought this is federal land, and you don't have jurisdiction here?"

"I'm a tribal cop," he said. He sounded angry. I figured that if I did not follow him I would effectively be on the run from the law. I sighed and told him I would go with him in his car.

He took me into his car and drove to the county jail. I wanted to ask why it was county, if he was emphasizing being all tribal, but the point was apparently lost on him and the system. I guess they had a deal. What was strange, though, was the ice-blue gaze of the policeman. It was Rosella's boyfriend, I realized. I was beginning to feel more certain that I was losing my mind as we approached the jail. We were approaching it due to a misunderstanding with my landlord. I thought we had come to some sort of agreement, but we hadn't, and she enforced the lease, and so it came to be that I was now with a famous singer's secret boyfriend, a towering redhead who picked me up on my way to a meat-pie-making activity. Was that why Rosella had been interested in me? Because I was crazy? Or was that why she had lost interest in me, because she discovered I was crazy? The jail was now less than a block away. He held me by the elbow as we walked. I felt like he was my date.

"You have the right to remain silent," he began.

"For my one call, I would like to talk to your girlfriend. She and I just collaborated on some songs together."

"I bet you did." He smirked and let his nostrils flare. I wanted to call him *cowboy*.

I said, "She has my number. I have hers."

He spat on the ground. Then, he escorted me into the first of four industrially locked anterooms. After the last vaulted room, we entered the arrestee check-in area. A balding man behind shatterproof glass held my gaze until a bobbed guard with matte burgundy almond-shaped nails rolled my fingers atop the glass of a large machine with the deftness of a manicurist. She asked my name, social security number, address, and such. Rosella's boyfriend went into the hall and made a call, staring at me the whole time.

"Do you know Mike?" the bobbed guard asked.

"No," I said.

Mike opened the giant door. "It's for you."

"Who is it?" I asked.

He held out the phone. Somehow, I did not believe it would be Rose. I took it.

"Hello?" she said in that soft girl-cry tone. A cockroach moved around the toe of my hot-pink tennis shoe.

"Hi," I said. I was at a loss of words.

"So, did you ever find that eyeliner?"

"I thought it was eyeshadow." I laughed.

Mike glared. "Get to the point," he said. "Quickly."

"Why are cops always grouchy, especially boyfriend cops?" I said.

"Because they get butt-hurt when they act like asses and get broken up with."

"Oh."

"So you're in jail? For breaking a lease?"

"Yeah. And deserting the premises, failing to pay, letting pipes freeze, and overall breaking the contract."

Mike held a finger at me like *don't mess this up*. I wondered which of all Rose's hair colors he liked best. Probably the darker shade of black with matching nails or the faded carrot blond of her earlier Nancy Sinatra style.

"You're done," said Mike.

"Gotta go," I said.

The officer took my wrist, no longer gentle, and led me toward the room of the balding man who hated me with his eyes. We turned left and he put me in the smallest room in the inner square of the jailhouse. I was peaceful, and folded both of my arms to lie on my stomach on the bench. Hours later I woke to Rose in a purple dress with a plunging neckline, her extra ten pounds looking Oklahoma perfect and her hair bouncy and big, heavy rollers fresh out.

The door was open and there she stood, half smiling, half squint-eyed skeptical, like I was a rescue animal she wasn't sure about.

Rose comes onto the stage She has only six songs. I watch her profile. She's great. Outside it's a full moon and we aren't drinking, so we walk the boulevard. In Hollywood, there is the sound of other bands playing. Some meth heads gesture at the sky near a fire hydrant and a Native dude in a do-rag tries to pick us up. I don't think he recognizes Rosella. He drives beside us and we pretend to talk on my phone for two blocks, but really it is just the dude asking again and again, "Do you need a ride, do you need a ride?" He has Comanche plates and he is attractive. Rose and I go home as soon as he tires of following us and does a screeching U-turn. We sit in her living room and sing covers, but we do not finish the song. The next day she has to leave for Europe and asks me to house-sit. I say yes, because I am homeless. She messages me from Dublin, Berlin, Copenhagen. I sit by her pool and stare at a dogwood that, in the course of my visit, goes from white to green. I play her piano and sing in G, though I can't remember the words the minute they leave my mouth, and no one is around to hear.

THE WIFE
𐓇𐒰𐒼'𐓂́

It was raining in Berkeley the day I received the call that my father was about to die. Outside my kitchen window, two men took shelter under a covered patio behind a pizza joint. My mother cried on the phone as I watched the men. They were smoking, sitting on a bench.

"He's going into surgery now," my mother said.

I'd been grading, and moved the stack of papers away. "Thanks for letting me know. Would you call again when you have news?"

She whimpered, but I felt nothing. It was my father's third time dying. The first time, he contracted MRSA shaving his bone-dry face with a rusty razor during one of his campouts in our backyard—a habit I barely registered as strange at seventeen; everything he did was strange to me, and I was too busy trying to avoid him to think about his behavior at any length. His doctor told us that my father had twenty-four hours to live. The sore on his neck was covered when I entered the hospital room with the last book I thought we'd discuss.

He took it weakly, crying quiet tears. It was *The Call of the Wild* by Jack London, which follows a dog named Buck who lives in a feral state, half dog, half wolf, and rejected by all. Doubtless my father identified, being of mixed Native and European descent. But he did nothing to gain acceptance. When our tribe offered him a building job in Oklahoma, he turned it down because it was a thousand dollars below his minimum. He reminded me of the way Native studies professors spoke of Coyote, as the archetype of a person who thought he was more important than other people, and therefore became a trickster resorting to tricking even himself. My father often tricked me, too, but I grieved like he would really die.

My husband entered our third-floor apartment with a creak of the door, but I barely acknowledged him. I had a timer on and was grading five papers an hour. The phone rang, and my brother's image came across the screen. He was serious in the photo, with his work belt slung around his hips, left foot raised out of a foundation he was digging, as though about to step out, fling the belt off, and quit forever. He was my father's foreman, after years of college but not enough humility to work his way up, careerwise, in science jobs.

The phone kept ringing.

John hugged me. "What's going on?"

I realized I was crying from the taste sliding down the back of my throat, salt water thick with mucus, slow like blood.

I shook my head and went to the window. The men on break in the parking lot wore boots, lace-up Wolverines. Their feet tapped. I answered the phone.

"Are you coming here?" asked my brother.

"I don't know," I said. "How is she?"

He said she was fine, and gave the phone to her.

My mother breathed heavily. "I don't know," she began, "why you wouldn't want to see your father when you don't know what will happen!"

The timer on my phone went off in a ricochet of bells.

"I am a worm, a wretch!" my mother said.

"What?" I snoozed the timer. "What are you talking about?"

"I yelled at your dad, right before it happened!"

"Mom," I said. People at my childhood church often said she was possessed, mostly because she suffered constant headaches that she refused to acknowledge as migraines, I think out of fear of my father saying she exaggerated. She would never let them cast out the demon, and insisted on being respected by everybody, perhaps to her detriment. I wanted her to go into therapy, and to cry for once. It seemed her whole existence was based off a constant denial.

When I turned away from the window, John was gone, and I was alone with my mom's hard breathing. She'd told us once that going to traditional dances was pagan, but her mom was Creole, a mixed girl whose mother left New Orleans and married a German, and by her New Orleans ancestry, she was as pagan as I was.

"Let's talk after dinner," I said.

"Fine." She erupted in one of her coughing fits, which meant she'd put milk in her tea.

We got off the phone and I put carrots on a cutting board. I thought randomly of the time John shoved me into the fridge during a fight. I told him if he ever hit me again, I'd leave. And he hadn't ever hit me again. My father used to hit us with a board he kept beside the bed, but he never left bruises or injured us. Instead he left us in the room for hours, until we performed a convincing but insincere apology, or spanked me bare-bottomed until I broke down in hysterics.

I put on my rain jacket and went outside to the red bench. The workers were gone. The slatted blinds of our kitchen contrasted with the dark blue sky. There were still things I wanted from my father, like clarity on my identity. During my teen years, my AOL screen name was Ogeese7, assigned by my dad in honor of an ancestor, but I knew few of our traditions. It was humiliating, having a moniker like that while attending a Baptist school teaching us that NDNs were all dead.

I went inside and forced myself to cook, eat, and wash. Then I fell asleep. Eventually John started playing the guitar. I woke to his thin, womanly voice singing that one person had taken all his feeling. He looked at me while he sang, but I knew better than to attribute a look like that to real attention. It had taken me years to really comprehend that the player's mind is focused on the complex task of singing, remembering, and moving their fingers.

My mother called again. It was nine. I declined the call and got my old copy of *The Call of the Wild*, then bought a plane ticket and left, just like that. John seemed to know I was going, or else he didn't care. I took the bus to the airport with great numbness, enacting my usual travel fast, to cultivate a low burning hunger that helped me cope with the numbness. After the first flight, on a three-hour layover I drank a black coffee. The second flight was brief, landing just after dawn. Then I got a rental car and went straight to the hospital. It was a short drive, and the numbers and letters of the license plates on the cars I followed seemed to leer at me. I reached the hospital at 8 a.m. and wandered the bright halls until I found my father sleeping in a powder-blue room, his hands resting on his chest, remnants of drool crusted on his mouth. My mother and brother were nowhere to be seen.

I squeezed his foot gently.

"Anna!" he said, waking in a gasp.

I held out the Jack London book and he took it and opened it up. "*Chapter one, Into the Primitive.*" He laughed and breathed quietly. "I always wished you lived with us," he said as he met my eye. "I want you to live with your mother, or take her to live with you."

He expected people to respond emphatically to grandiose statements, but I was tired of pretending. I said nothing. He interpreted my silence as a sign I wasn't doing well, and immediately started in with his typical advice, which centered around running metaphors: "When you get tired, you need to rely on your form. I told you to hold crackers in your fingers when you run, run on your toes, always stand in ready position and lean forward, breathe in through your nose and out through your mouth. One thing you have never learned is how to rest. I told you when you get tired, rely on your form. You're like your mother. You need to know when to rest."

I nodded in agreement. He wasn't wrong. Now it was my turn to tell him something: "I'm preoccupied with why I'm alive," I said.

His gaze was neutral, so I pressed on. "The first thing I think when I wake every day is 'Is this still going?' As in any of it? I remember when it started. I couldn't do anything without questioning how it worked and trying to break it down into the smallest pieces—if I turned on the radio, I would think about sound waves and how they worked, trying to understand the mechanism of a dial and how it all was connected. None of it makes sense." I was surprised he was still listening. I began to talk faster. "The same thing with me, you know? How's all this *really* happening?" I said, looking down at myself.

He sighed. "You would have been happier skipping college and starting that horse farm."

The mountain range of white peaks blinked with the sunrise out the window. I felt like a milk carton that had been filled up with water, shaken, and emptied. My father took my hand and squeezed it.

I said, "I read in the Bible not to be afraid of bad news."

"That's hard. Let me read aloud to you," he said, holding up the Jack London.

"Do you want anything to eat first?"

"No."

"Let me just get some tea. I'll be right back."

I slipped out and ran down the steps, hoping for a vending machine, but instead I discovered my mother eating packaged oatmeal over a small Formica table in a corner of the cafeteria. She gave a little cry and hugged me, all at once, while clearing her teeth of oatmeal. The sound was strangely comforting. My brother leaned back. His presence calmed me. At six feet, three inches, he was draped over his chair like a cool, casual panther.

"Can I get you some food?" my mother asked. "Get anything you like."

"No, nothing. What do the doctors say?"

"We don't know yet. Want to go up there?" my mother asked.

"I saw him already."

There was no tea. I got myself a cup of burned coffee and told them I would sit there and wait a bit. The few nurses in the cafeteria followed my mother and brother out of the room, and in that free space my mind wandered. I imagined my mother like a single mom with three children, one of whom she loved and married. My father had never made a cent of profit in his business, and evaded his taxes. The IRS came to our house and tried to take their car, but my mother's family bailed them out of trouble. My brother and I had to work even more so we could avoid foreclosure, and they never got their finances stable. When I married, my parents removed $6,000 from my savings.

If he was finally dead, I thought, that would be a burden off me. This thought triggered an uncanny sensation I knew too well. The last time it happened, the world had fractalized, the moments before me breaking off into little splinters, so that if I tried to stand up or put a thing in a box (like I had while moving into our Berkeley apartment with John), my brief actions felt like they were happening over hours. It was not yet proper psychosis, but it wasn't a healthy mind, either. I closed my eyes and waited for the uncanny feeling to dissipate, and when it diminished, I tossed my coffee in the trash. I found a bathroom just outside the cafeteria, and in the mirror, I noticed that my right eyebrow was drooping down, toward my eyelid. Spots blanketed my vision. An infinity of them, swarming like bees.

I thought of the second time my father didn't die, after a stroke while traveling spontaneously to play a song for a musician he knew in Nashville. The right half of his face sank after the stroke, and he was left with a blank, flaccid expression in the hospital bed for days after. But he recovered. It was not dissimilar to the face he wore while watching sports on TV at night: vacant, marble-hard eyes. It was the same one he wore when our neighbor came into the house and wrestled me into a hug, grabbed my breasts, and wouldn't let go. I fought that neighbor, and won, because I was stronger. After my grandmother told my mom what happened, she said his meds were off. Then my dad encouraged me to wear my bikini on the riding lawn mower. I felt like a motorcycle chick, riding with "Daddy," except he was really, actually, my father. The neighbor who'd attacked me watched the show from his front stoop as I bounced on the mower.

With the tips of my fingers I dabbed at the slackened side of my face as I got in the elevator to go back up to my father, but I didn't push the button. The doors opened, closed, and reopened, but I didn't move. My mother called. I declined.

I texted John. *Come here?*

I don't know, he texted back.

John had never wanted to meet any of my friends, the way I had with his. They were young-hearted and innocent people. He was so different from the boys I'd known growing up, sons of small-time farmers and packing-plant workers who took six-packs on small boats and went fishing. John's purity of heart, his perhaps naive idealism, struck me. I had known boys as pushing me to be sexually aggressive, advocates of sunset hide-and-seek; or dangerous, urging me to try their various drugs; or superior, giving me books to read and advice on how to dress, date, be. John was smart but respectful and conservative in a way that still fit my southern Christian upbringing. John had liked me because I was sensitive and felt so much, but at a certain point he'd told me not to share tears and feelings with him too much, because he had no space for them. I'd started holding back, and we'd never found a happy medium.

I left the hospital, got in the car, and sped, but I wasn't sure where I was going. I stopped at a gas station and parked, watching the reflection of my rental car in the convenience store window. It was black, like my old truck, and felt safe. I avoided looking at my face in the mirror—the spots persisting. Constellating between them I saw the glimpse of my old self, the one my father had loved. The way they had raised me, there was not supposed to be room for me. But something had changed. I was different, and in the process of becoming my own person, delayed as I was in beginning to do so, by the insular and strict nature of my childhood.

For most of my childhood, my father had been someone to be beautiful for, who would watch me closely and admire me. I wore my mother's dresses and we went on father-daughter dates. As I grew older, the waitresses assumed that I was his wife. I pictured myself standing under a continual rain of sawdust from my father's Husqvarna saw, blinding me, choking me.

I called John again, but he didn't pick up. Would he care that I was potentially having a stroke? I checked return flights online, but they were all expensive. I called him again, to ask what our price range was. But it was useless. He kept his phone on silent whenever he was asleep or at work. I fantasized about leaving him, but I saw myself homeless and living in a car; and even that was unrealistic because he owned the car. Even though I had a job, I felt helpless. The last time I had gone home after a trip, John had cried and said he'd been happier when I was away. He said he hadn't loved me since we were nineteen, which I'd known, but hearing it really hurt. We'd married as soon as I got to college, after my father told me I would always do what he said, and that he would always own me until I was married; but that he would still own me because eventually my husband would get "over me" and I'd have to come back to him. I often wondered if he would be right, since it became clear early on in the marriage that my way of doing things irritated John. When we went to a party of a mutual friend and encountered snobby grad students, I made jokes and asked questions until everyone got to talking about themselves. The host thanked me for making it a great party, but John said it was disgusting, how I had to be the center of attention.

My brain tingled with disbelief. Was this what it felt like for my father? A neurologist told him he had a male anger pattern—otherwise known as rage—to thank for his suffering. I needed to do something to make myself feel better. I ran into the gas station and bought a zero-calorie Gatorade and a pack of Flamin' Hot Cheetos. I texted my mom that a work emergency had come up and I would have to leave. Then I sat in the gas station parking lot and searched my phone for clues about what to do.

I looked at my Notes app and saw one file titled "Wife Score." I opened it, and read what I no longer remembered having written.

WIFE SCORE: 90

The wife rates highest in the categories of sex and general mood and receives extra points for participating in the partner's preferred leisure activities The wife rates lowest in the categories of meal preparation consistency and general emotional stability The wife initiates sex and tries all suggested sexual positions If struck, the wife will vacate the physical proximity of the

> partner regardless of circumstances and location The wife has general eating habit abnormalities The wife reports low blood sugar The wife is not prone to jealousy The wife expects the partner to cook intermittently The wife recycles The wife is moderately clean The wife vacuums, does dishes, cleans the bathroom The wife refuses to unload grocery bags The wife is not skilled at taxes The wife will refrain from moving the partner's things The wife will handle customer service issues The wife will earn money The wife will follow the budget The wife can be persuaded to do laundry The wife tolerates the partner's participation in some weeknight activities The wife is prone to same-sex friendships The wife has ironed shirts twice The wife has a high exuberance level The wife enjoys dancing singing swimming running boxing The wife is better at basketball than tennis but will try any sport one-on-one except golf The wife is prone to a weak sense of self The wife enjoys the extra attention of manipulators The wife enjoys jumping through hoops to please a manipulative partner The wife is not prone to flirtation

John called and I picked up quick. "Hello," he said.

"I miss you," I said.

He said nothing.

"I wasn't going to come home, if you don't want me to."

"That seems premature," he said.

"Oh. Do you still love me?" I laughed at myself for asking this. It was something my father told me his mother repeatedly asked him.

But John wasn't laughing. He let out a huge sigh, and I worried he was going to cry again and say he hated me. But he said that of course he loved me. He said I was his best friend. "You know," he continued, "I really just wish that we had stayed best friends instead of getting married."

I didn't know what to say. I had never felt that way about him. He didn't go with me to museums or concerts or get coffee or enjoy traveling like a best friend might, and he wanted me to be a smaller person, to feel less and be less out in the world. I had grown up without friends, mostly because my father could be very frightening. He once tore down a room framed out by two-by-fours while my brother stood beneath the falling wood beams.

"I'm sorry," I said. "I want to come home. But the flights are expensive." I said this in an attempt to ask permission to use what I thought of as his money.

"How is your dad?" he said.

"I don't know. He's really sick." I started to cry.

"Maybe stay there?" he said. "I know it's hard. But I don't want you to regret anything."

I thought of John, wet with rain, his shirt clinging to his arms but loose around his torso. I thought of the molding bowl of soup on his desk. He wasn't that great at taking care of himself. Out the window of my rental car there was a woman hurrying through the parking lot, hunched over a sloshing coffee cup. Two men left the convenience store and pulled beers out of their pockets. One lifted the aluminum can to me, a toast. I lowered my head and touched my face, not wanting to look in the mirror.

"Anna?" my husband asked.

I started at the sound of my name and gasped.

He laughed. "I haven't heard your death breath in a while."

"I love you," I told him, and then I really began to cry as my options became apparent.

I could go back to the hospital, and wait, and grade more papers. I could dial my mother and ask her not to yell at me. I could feel nothing and dissociate. I could make plans to move away. I could wait and do nothing. I could cry so hard I would fall into a black hole, but I also felt (possibly?) capable enough to step over such-and-such void that my English-major friends and I had aestheticized for years. But I didn't want to aestheticize my death, not if I could drive and walk carefully out of the parking lot and into the hospital and sit in the room and say goodbye to my father forever.

"I want to cry now," I told John. "But I'll go, because I just want to make sense."

He was quiet, but I heard him swallow. I got off the phone without either of us saying anything more. When I went back to the hospital after that, I didn't hold my dad's hand. I asked my mom to hold it, and at first she said she didn't like touching people, but when she saw my face, she gave me a look I had only ever seen from my grandmother. It was a knowing look void of fakeness and denial, and it was a great gift that she made that expression. I knew, as she grabbed my father's hand, that she would not comment on my face, or on anything, and though she could not do any more than offer me silence, it was enough to feel seen by her.

"I need to tell John I'm moving out," I said. And I began to cry.

My mom nodded in understanding, and she asked if I wanted to hear about heart attack diets. "Just, if it's too much to talk about, you know," she said.

I understood her limits, and I agreed. She talked about sweet potatoes, broccoli, beans, and the healthy habits of centenarians; after all, we were all here because of a heart attack. My mom mentioned genes, and I thought of my father's sisters.

"Auntie Lillie eats like that, doesn't she?" I said. "I could call her."

"Yes," she said. "And after that, I understand if you have to go."

I hugged her, and she let me. In the mirror, I noticed my face had corrected itself.

FULL TILT

1957

When Lora got Florence's call about the search warrant, she was on the garage love seat blasting her pedicure dry in front of the new portable Magicoal Electric Fire heater. She watched the driveway, made of gravel, covered with broken-down cars forever awaiting repairs.

"Lorelai, why is there a policeman at my house?"

She feigned ignorance: "Did you steal something, Mother?"

"No. He says you did."

Her mother's voice went shrill in a tirade about joyriding, burning letters, search warrants. Lora held the phone away. A warrant was welcome news. It was a legitimate excuse to get out of North Carolina. She needed time off, and her man would not give it to her, but he couldn't argue with the law. It had taken her entire twenty-dollar paycheck, with the baby clutching and pulling her tops out of place, to afford the heater. Everett could let the baby clutch on to him for a week. Then maybe he wouldn't make her be cosupervisor for minimum wage because she was "slowed down."

"Mother?"

"—Your court date, says here, is October first. So I guess I'll finally get to meet Mina."

"Her name is Lucy."

"It's what we call a first daughter."

"We?"

"Osages."

"Oh. Well, she can't come. The drive down is too long. She'll have to stay with Everett."

"She needs to be with her mother. You bring her. And bring your new man. I always thought it was foolish when women married someone who didn't love them as much or more in return, but now that woman is me. So I'll have to learn from you. I waited for a half hour while that policeman searched the house for clues, drank my tea and his, then made two cups out of nervousness while he turned over every bit of paper. But he didn't search the fireplace."

"That truck was a parting gift from Charlie," Lora said simply. "It was *not* stolen."

"Well, he did leave it at the house, but I was never clear on him 'giving' it to you." An electric whir and clang of metal hummed. "Did I tell you I got Michael back? You can probably hear him playing. I'm meeting with the lawyer on Monday to figure out next steps if Jim challenges."

"Mother, I'll be there on Monday. Give Michael a hug for me."

"I will. Now, you be careful, hear?"

"Yes, Mother."

She lifted the needle off the record and got Lucy from her crib. She was still sleeping despite all the blondes at the beauty parlor next door shrieking at parrot decibels through the plywood walls. She strapped Lucy into the buggy and put her Dalida / Miss Egypt record back on in the living room and baked a cake black as hell, Blackest Day Cake with éclair ganache, the whole thing glazed until it was smooth as wet mud after a storm.

She had Frito pie ready as Everett came in. "Turn the music off, goddam it. It's so loud."

"Well, hi to you, too," she said, but Everett walked straight through the living room and into the bedroom as Dalida's voice rang through the room loud as a trombone on her final note. Lora danced the last beats, imitating the women who came into the furniture shop holding in their stomachs and taking small steps, but Everett clicked the door shut. Those women were exactly like the light maple polyurethane wash in the furniture store, their cheery personas all for show, everything about them trying to seem nonthreatening, but Dalida had a resonant voice like cherry mahogany, deep and dark and powerful. Lora loved that Dalida had both won Miss Universe and made an album in French. She cut the cake with a huff and poured herself red wine and changed into a floor-length velvet dress in the laundry room.

Lucy woke crying and Everett yelled, "Give 'er a bottle!" through the thin wood wall. She decided to go to the salon rather than risk getting Everett angrier. The mirrors and chatter kept Lucy calm, and Lora was happy to get her hair teased high for the drive to Oklahoma. She'd get as far as her Tennessee gas station on the other side of the Mississippi for a morning barbecue sandwich with a slice of apple pie, crinkly and grease-licked and tin-foil-wrapped by the old man with the unintelligible Memphis accent in the sweet rising fog over Arkansas grass. She felt her own mojo and she was going to rub it all across the South, starting now, with beauty queen hair.

Everett entered the reception area. "A word."

He grabbed her hand and pulled her, and because she didn't want a scene in front of the salon, she let him pull her all the way up the steps and back into the apartment. Everett got her in the door and took Lucy from her, set the baby down, and out of nowhere punched Lora right in the face.

"I heard that French whore music and I see your skinny little whore toes and your tight little dress and the hair, and why are you making that cake—what the hell has got into you!"

Other people's rage made her calm and sharp, an old counter-reflex to her mother. "I got a search warrant for joyriding. I've got to see my mother."

Everett's jaw cracked open delicate as an egg, because he didn't think she was capable of *evil* like he was, but yes, maybe if she positioned herself as the criminal he would back down.

But his face widened in rage. "You stole a goddamn *car*?"

The shock in her face turned to a throb. It was hard to believe this was really happening. She felt numb, and touched her chin with the point of her nail. On her finger, there was blood.

The sight of it made her angry, and her anger made her think very fast. "Look, genius, me and this baby, we're going on a trip." It was obvious she couldn't leave him at this emotional location, so she would talk him down. "I don't know why you think I'm cheating on you, but you've given me a shiner to cover, so if you don't want to give me a kiss, why don't you get the hell out of my walking path and we won't talk until I'm back and I find you on your bruised-up, gravel-covered knees begging for my love or else I'm gone for good, you sucker-punching ass."

Everett smiled, all catlike. "This is my house. You're sleeping in *my bed* tonight, and you're not going anywhere."

"Seeing as you may not comprehend, I'll inform you that I am going because that cute little truck we drove out here after yours broke down on the side of the road? You know, in that cute ditch at that Nowata bar? That car was from my ex. So we are going to return it, seeing as he also experienced memory loss and forgot he gave it to me begging and crying, just like you should be, and—let me tell you what, I am not going to work another goddamn second at your glorified mattress shop. If you try to hit me and punch me dead, good for you, do it, I'll just wake up, sit up, stand up sometime when you're sleeping and I'll put the entire contents of the house into the back of my truck because I'm the Daisy Mae, I am an Amazon, you are nothing and you won't stop me. I'll leave sooner or later, so get your dick out of your asshole and sit down and eat a piece of cake or else go drink. I don't care, just step off me because I'm not minimum wage. You are."

She didn't feel angry. She just knew how to turn it on, and it seemed she'd overfilled his brain like detergent in the washer because he just breathed loud through his nose while she flipped the Dalida and step-ball-changed to the beat and threw dresses into a bag and found the roll of cash under her side of the mattress and scooped the baby and got in the car. She loved a fresh start, and knew she was so tough that her pain level was primed for United States military torture. She revved the engine once but had to cut it because she'd forgotten her cosmetics. With the car idling she ran up and threw them all into a clean trash bag and took the whole damn cake, too, except one piece.

Everett was motionless in the doorway. She held her red fingernails against his brassy auburn hair and figured the whole thing might go off better if she seemed like she was changing her mind. Give him the feeling it wasn't real, that it was too fast. She pulled him around to the La-Z-Boy, his prize possession, and sat on his lap and pouted her lower lip big and shoved it into his mouth. When he began to suck on it like a pacifier she put her tongue in there and she really, really felt it: his salt taste and his feminine-soft earlobes in her fingers and she sucked at him too and she let him carry her to the bed and hitch the dress up and go on top like she liked because it was so much of a relief to not have control of absolutely everything for one second and it was kind of slow, like they were in love, and no matter how much she kissed him it was like she was drinking hot salted chocolate from his mouth. She sucked him down and ate him up and when he rolled off and slept she spat him out in the sink and drove while Lucy slept in the passenger seat.

When she got to B-ville, David John was scrambling an egg, and Vera was watching from the breakfast table with her weekend bag sitting on the opposite chair like she was at a café and not at her own home with her own room right down the hall.

"Wild, how we end up being home the same weekend," said Vera. "I was thinking my boyfriend would get to meet Mother alone and hopefully have less to deal with, but I guess not."

When she'd pulled up in her ex's truck, Vera had been in the driveway, too, and in the shuffle of bags into the house they'd let in a chirping cicada.

"My god, does it always have to be a zoo around here?" Vera had cried.

Lora knew how her sister hated this house, their family, and especially *her*. She was probably thinking of her right now as *fat*, what with her also breading chicken to fry it, but Lora actually pitied her sister, who had no behind, a flat chest, and wore too little makeup. In her corset, she felt that her narrow waist made her body look appealing, and she was grateful she was the sister with the darker hair and a flair for the dramatic. In the kettle, she winked at herself and admired her darkly winged eyes, black eyeliner swiped on like Dalida's. Against her coffee from the gas station, her nails were long and painted a red as dark as half-dried blood.

Vera was still watching. "Gas station coffee? From Dark Sky?" She read the Styrofoam cup. "That's awful stuff."

"I'm going to go slick my hair." David John sensed danger, and clattered off in his cherry-red cowboy boots.

"Take Lucy with you," said Lora.

"Oh, really! I didn't think you'd let me babysit."

"You're responsible, aren't you?"

"You bet I am."

All three went to the carrier sitting in the doorway, where light from the window caught the peach fuzz on the baby's fragile skin.

It was Vera who had to spoil the moment. "Whatever you're helping Florence with, she's at peak crazy. I don't even know what she's on. I spoke to her the other day on the phone, and, apparently, she married a man named Johnny B. Jack, who was her carpenter when she was with Jim. Who knows what drugs she's taking, half the time tranquilized, half the time sobbing, and she can't even function. She should go back to the institution, if you ask me."

David John picked up Lucy and escaped out of the kitchen quickly, and in that moment, she saw her sister seeing the moon-sliver curve of purple under Lora's eye.

Vera gasped. "My god! He's hitting you?"

"Try to keep the delight out of your voice, and lower it. I don't want David John to hear."

A burst of wind through the window fluttered papers sitting on top of the kitchen table.

Vera went after them. Lora put some water on to boil. "Now, if I make you some tea, we can sit down and talk about this."

"I don't think you should move in here, it's not a good idea," said Vera.

"Shetho^. Kitsea. Put those papers down under one of Mother's rocks and stop bossing."

"Every time I see you, it feels like we're meeting for the first time, or you've turned into a new kind of space alien. I feel like Gerald is more my family than you all are, but I still hope you'll like him when he comes to visit. He's so correct and smooth. You can actually predict what he will say, always something kind, reasonable, and in support of me."

Lora watched the whitish-blue truck glint in the moonrise. That old truck, faded the color of a storm cloud—the alleged parting gift from Lucy's father, the cheater.

Since Lora was giving her no response, Vera changed the subject. "So that ex-boyfriend of yours, are you going to get back with him now?"

"Why would I?"

"Isn't that why you're here?"

"No." Lora washed a random fork in the sink. "There's a warrant out, apparently. Charlie says he forgot he gave me the car, I suppose. She wants it back. Why wouldn't she?"

"Are you telling me… Wait, I don't understand. What happened, exactly?"

Vera was probably guessing theft, jail, yelling-fighting—her sister's "trashy lifestyle" offering dramas better than television soap operas.

"If *your* ex-boyfriend gave *you* his girlfriend's car, it's your stupidity that has to go to jail," said Vera. "You really can't just trust anyone. Maybe you need to stop being so naive."

Lora's face finally went flat, all the air escaping from it like a blow-up pool toy. "Yes, Charlie gave me his girlfriend's car, but I thought it was his car. And I'm attending to that. Maybe *you* need to mind your own business. Have you ever thought of that?"

David John came in holding Lucy. "Look. She has teeth." Bite marks covered his arm.

"Good god," said Vera. "Why did you let her do that?"

David John shrugged. "It was interesting."

"Please don't curse, Vera." Lora got a cloth and put it on David's arm. "Set her down, and go wash. She was born with those teeth, and she knows how to use them."

David John obeyed, but stole away some little cookies on a tea plate to take with him.

Both sisters watched, and they couldn't help but laugh. Florence entered in a pink silk robe, and she did not see David John's arm under the cloth.

She went to her grandchild. "Wichoshpa," Florence said.

The women kissed each other on the cheeks. "I didn't know if I'd ever get my girls back at once," Florence said.

The kettle faltered into a whistle, then a scream.

Lora turned the heat off and moved it away, then faced her mother. "I want to stay here."

Vera saw a flash of yellow under the foundation of her sister's right cheekbone as she delivered the outlandish news that she was homeless, on the run from the law, and needed a hideout as well as shelter. Vera closed her eyes and realized she was fainting, as it happened.

When she woke up what seemed like a moment later, she was under a lace-trimmed quilt she'd never seen before.

"Sweetheart." Florence held a glass of lemon water. Pink gauze curtains behind her made her seem rosy and pale, like a doll.

"Is this your, your, his, uh, what's his name?"

"Johnny B. Jack? Yes. This is our guest room."

"What happened?" Automatic tears suddenly heated Vera's cheeks.

David John appeared through the semitranslucence of the curtains and she could just make him out, wheeling his bike into the driveway, gaping at the car, into the window, at her.

Florence yawned. "Lora went to the new record store in Tulsa."

"Surprising she has time for hobbies, getting beat on all the time."

"That's a horrible thing to say." Florence rubbed the top of her left hand with two fingers and said some incomprehensible phrases that sounded something like the sounds "P" and "G" as in the film *Gigi.* It was Osage, apparently. She had never understood her mother's ridiculous affects and mannerisms, and even the thought of being there another hour gave her a headache.

"It's just that I thought Lora wasn't all that interested in music. You know I don't sugarcoat."

"She's just having a hard time."

Vera made to sit up, but her heart fluttered and she fell back. "Who cares about Lora, what happened to me?"

"You just fainted. The house was stuffy."

"Why don't you have air-conditioning? Maybe Johnny B. Jack can install it," Vera said, and the picture of it made her laugh out loud, despite the tears. They heard the front door squeak. Johnny B. Jack, Florence's third husband, did not have the prowess to soothe a creaking front door, much less install air-conditioning. Vera needed water, but she needed to see Gerald even more. She downed the lemon water and kicked herself out from under the covers. She would not be caught in this net of drama. Why should she be around women with broken pickers? Women who picked inept men and batterers?

Vera was worth more, but her mother couldn't accept it. As she sat up to go, Florence pressed needy fingers on her. "Stay for dinner, won't you?"

"All the gravy and biscuits, steak and gravy, gravy and fried chicken would not keep me here. Mother, I've been meaning to tell you. I'm in love. His name is Gerald. I'm going to have him take me to the doctor. I need to get checked out for my fainting. I just came to say Gerald would like to visit for Thanksgiving and meet y'all. Also, I wish you luck with the legal affairs."

"Hold on one minute. I have to tell you something."

"I have a statistics paper due tomorrow. I would also like to visit the doctor today, so pardon me for heading out."

"But I want to get you on a plane to France."

"You what?"

"Chief invited us to help plan the next cultural trip. I'd like to take you. You'd go free if you just do a bit of work, a call or two, no more than a high school club."

"I don't want to talk about the price of oil or whatever you fight over. I have class."

A vision of Paris came to Vera. She wore a breezy picnic sheet dress among tulips.

Florence handed Vera her hat. "You've gained weight. A trip could walk it off. You'd just miss a week of class. You can do that, can't you?"

"I've gained weight? What about Lora?" Vera knew she was 126 pounds and, last she checked, still five foot six.

"Lora has a full figure—yours is more like mine. We don't hold weight like she can."

"I'm going home to study and then see a doctor. I'll let you know how my health is, if you care to remember. Good night."

She met Lora in the driveway examining the front of a red album.

"You went out cold. Are you okay?"

"I'm not sure. But being here is not healthy."

"Did Mother ask you to go to France? She asked me while you were asleep."

"You mean passed out cold," she corrected. "Yes. And I hope you know that's not how to travel. What'd you get?"

"For Mother." Lora slid out a sleeve that read *RCA Victor* in huge letters, then "Heartbreak Hotel." Elvis. She complimented Vera's bracelet, a small sterling silver chain. "I bet Mother loved that. She loves anything silver."

"Gerald gave it to me."

"Fancy. Does he know you're Indian?"

"My god! The delusions around here. Are they giving you free health care or something?"

"No. Why?"

"Do you think anyone is going to believe you're Indian? Do you see Florence dancing around in moccasins?"

Lora shrugged.

"Oh my god. Mother is mixed-blood. What does that make you, an eighth? Aunt Blanche warned me about this poor-

Indian thing. Mother was raised in wealth. That Catholic school was the finest. Give it up already." Vera's hands flew up like a mime's inside a glass box, but she whipped them down just as fast and got into her car, which actually belonged to Gerald. "We got colonized, you know. They *won*. The Euros."

"So what are you?"

"Pardon me?"

"You said 'they.'"

"I may be the descendant of a chief, but I am not an Indian. And that 'chief'? He is not a chief. They're *colonized*. The Europeans *won*. Don't try to trap me in that story, Lora. That's Florence's story, it's got nothing to do with me. And don't go around telling everyone you're a quarter or an eighth or whatever it is."

She slammed the door, started the car up, and backed it out slowly before screeching off. Could someone explain to her how she was related to these people? They made her lose time. Gerald would be waiting at the park with McDonald's. He'd ask if she'd eaten anything and lift the curled ends of her hair behind her shoulders and she'd ask him if he'd gotten her a Coke and burger and he'd say yes and comment that it was cold out, and then offer her his jacket.

She admired her thin hand on the steering wheel as she drove, and parked in the last open guest spot near Gerald's dorm.

He was waiting beneath a baby oak tree. "There she is!"

Lora walked back into the house angry, hot like piss in a cup.

David John was choking over a skillet of smoking bacon.

She opened the windows and lifted the fork he'd been using to groom the edges of a blackening egg. He pointed to cold, burned toast. When Lora was his age they had been too poor for a toaster.

"Don't you know how to scrape burned toast, kid?" She pulled a chair to the sink and showed him how to shear the toast, then he smeared jam on it and ate half.

"Let's check on Lucy," she said.

She was in the back of the truck making *ee* vowel sounds.

David John pointed at her teeth. "Does it hurt when she drinks from your elbow?"

Lora suppressed her laugh. "Let's go to the store."

They'd made it a block short of the Piggly Wiggly when they saw Charlie holding a pool cue and spitting chew into a flowerpot outside Copper's. A shopkeeper was chastising Charlie, who caught sight of her through the man's raised arms. Lora stopped the car to see, and for a moment, they were in the middle of the road.

"It's important to keep moving forward when you drive," David John said.

She hit her blinker and turned into a parking spot.

Charlie was staring at her dead in the face, standing over the huge flowerpot.

"We're not where we were going," David John stated. From the flatness in his voice, she could tell he recognized her ex, and he did not approve of any interaction between them.

David John got out of the car, and took Lucy out. He rocked her in his arms and got back in the front seat. It was sweet how he was signaling to Charlie that he needed to leave them alone, but she thought making the baby known was a mistake. Some men saw vulnerabilities as reasons to leave women well enough alone, and others saw opportunities.

Charlie stared, though, and he did not act. She couldn't understand why.

"Is he drunk?" David John asked. "It's like we're staring at a bull, and there's an invisible fence between us he knows about but we don't. I want to leave."

Lora slid silently out of the truck, telling David John to stay put. She didn't have time to explain what she was doing, even to herself. She was acting on pure intuition. The shopkeeper took notice of her and two women passed in matching burgundy skirts.

"This here is my former woman," said Charlie.

The shopkeeper squinted briefly at Lora.

"Guess Charlie here won't spit in your plant anymore," she said. "That right, Charlie?"

"Guess that depends."

"On what?" she asked.

The shopkeeper used a hand shovel to cover the mucus with dirt.

"You've filled out," Charlie said.

The women had stopped to smoke. They watched, and their presence seemed protective, neutralizing the risk of having David John and Lucy in the car. Lora felt safe.

Charlie chuckled. "That truck is mine," he said, slurring his *s*.

"It's your girl's truck, right?" she said. In verbal combat, she would give him a two out of ten. "As far as I can tell, I'm the one not drunk, behaving responsibly for the sake of children like the two I've got in the car. I'm clean, neat, and doing errands like a responsible person, whereas you are drunk and disorderly. Seems like I really deserve the car. Especially as you gave it to me, also drunk, as I can recall, while you, from the look of it, don't recall much at all."

Charlie whistled. "Ain't my car. Indian giver, eh?"

"That shopkeeper is about to run you out of here. I'm not stupid." She took a step toward him. "David John has your gun in the car, so don't fight or he'll shoot you."

He spat, again, into the plant and ran his tongue over his front teeth. His new girl had cowed him for her and he couldn't even stare right, he was looking past her.

She turned and saw DJ holding a gun. "Lora? Can I put it down?"

"Posthaste," Charlie muttered.

It didn't take more time than the snap of the glove box to figure out what to say to him. She spun back. "Mom said Johnny B. Jack doesn't love her and he's going to stay with her until David John is in college. Everyone gets their heart broken in this town, but that doesn't mean you have to be broke down. If you were half the man Johnny B. Jack was, you would offer me the car, much less ten years of your life. If you want, we can take ten years to settle about your girlfriend's car, by which I mean litigation, or you can decide to stop in for biscuits whenever, anytime, and call it peace."

"That ain't fair. You don't live here even," he said.

"But I do."

"That's ten years. I can stop by for ten years?"

"Forever. Drop the charges."

Charlie screwed the tip of the pool cue into the sidewalk. "I'll play you," he said, quiet.

"I don't think so." She turned to her brother and motioned downward with her hand, indicating that he should lower the gun. David John was a little shaky but lowered it with care. He must've set Lucy in the back before he cocked the gun, because she was out of sight. That was his good instinct, keeping the baby safe while using the threat of an actual shot to intimidate.

Charlie watched, mournful, then turned away and headed for the bar. Lora slowly backed the car out and turned it into the Piggly Wiggly lot a mere three hundred feet away.

Charlie's figure went inside the bar and did not return.

"He gave up," she said, and stared at Lucy, who watched from the floor with fascination.

David John stared at the gun and didn't say anything. It was pointed away from them.

"What is it? You did good. I'm going to take that thing from you now," she said.

David John didn't seem to hear her. "Mom has a trash life," he said.

"What?"

"Mom said she has a trash life." He looked at her accusingly.

"I'm moving back in anyway," she said. She reached over him and locked the safety.

He put the gun in the glove compartment. "Was it loaded?" he said.

"No," she lied. Adrenaline was coursing through her body like the Mississippi in flood. "Soon we'll be sitting at the table drizzling syrup over hot buttered stacks, so let's just calm down here and stop talking crap. The only trash life is being unable to get what you want, and what you need. Our mother doesn't have a regular way of thinking, but she is still a beautiful person, because she never stops trying to change and get her family what we need."

David John picked Lucy up. "I'm going to be a beautiful person, too," he said. He arranged her baby blanket around her like a shawl. "And I'm going to start with getting you what you need," he said.

"Little brother, you helped me just now, but I want you to understand that you do not need to take care of anyone except, eventually, one day, yourself. But right now, today, it's me who's going to take care of you. So when we go into that grocery store, you can pick one thing you request, but do not go on asking for everything in there, or I'm going to whoop you. Hear?"

HOUSE OF RGB

Death could not get a word in edgewise,
grew discouraged, and traveled on.
—Louise Erdrich, *Tracks*

I pulled up to the half-razed tree at the turn-in to 111 Infinity Drive and My Love walked out of the shade to give me a kiss, burping the scent of the lily-root soup I'd made for the ancestors.

"That soup was for Grandma Jane. The table was clean. I buy you expensive salmon dog food, and you still have to steal? I know you're a dog, but I need you to be classier than that."

My Love hopped into the car and turned his face toward me, reminding me of my former lover, named Julius. I could picture him settling into the passenger seat, instead of my elegant dog with this shiny black coat of short curls. Instead of silently listening to me, Julius would tap on the semihollow box of his phone, a poor listener in the light echo of lithium cobalt oxide as well as graphite anode, or perhaps tungsten and rare earth, those elements responsible for the brilliant reds, blues, and greens of the screen. His tapping always signaled his unavailability, and the vibrations of neodymium and dysprosium in his texts had triggered vibrations in my own skin that finally told me to leave him. So I had. I confessed to My Love that I missed Julius, and he made a dog murmur. We went inside, where I set my grocery bags down and spotted a note taped to the wall next to the jackets.

Take a hike to the beach

I had completely forgotten this note, though I'd written it last night in a bout of frustration after receiving another DM from a poet who drank so much that he had texted at 3:43 a.m., which is not to say he'd woken me up. As he texted to compliment me and complain about his relationship in one sentence, I was sitting on my hot-pink velvet couch while ancestors appeared to me wearing wire-rimmed glasses and encouraged me to flirt with him.

"Flirt with the poet?" I lit my pipe. "You are the daughter of the man who negotiated the Oklahoma sale of our current land from the Cherokees, and you are telling me to flirt."

I called them out sometimes, and had been tempted to turn my back on their advice.

I went back to the car and hustled the rest of the groceries from the sedan into the fridge before finally sitting down in front of my paused video game. My Love went to the screen, where an elfin Jane and a wizardly Tarzan were frozen atop a ledge, waiting to investigate the landscape as they clutched shoots of thick vine. I pressed a button and we shimmied down the cliff. (This is the thing we are supposed to do, and you are doing it, too, scaling down, needing something badly, down there, below, though we don't know what or why.)

After a while My Love placed his paw on my knee and gently coughed. This was a dog trained to make polite *ahem*s, because, as a girl, I had fantasized about mothering a regiment of six well-trained boys. Now, childless, I had only My Love to parent. It was time for us both to eat, but I told My Love to hold on. My avatar and her companion set foot at the bottom of a waterfall. Through the cascade of water, a dragon erupted in flight, emitting a shout that released a wave of sonic violence upon the characters. Our feet splashed up and our bodies floated, dead.

"We have to restart from before." I sighed. My Love gave a whistling whine and went to the windows to survey the ocean. "All right. Remember, I already packed our bags so this would be easy."

I poured tincture into my coffee. A Realtor friend had sent the tincture, which was supposed to help with chronic pain; it was called rose quartz essence, made by bathing flowers in moonlight and combining the resulting roseate liquid with vodka or gin and a pink quartz rock in a vial. Outside I sipped as we proceeded down the path, the air tasting of wild roses. The *medicinal* function of the tincture was alcoholic, and I had given a lot of thought to the question of ancient medicinal uses of tequila—purposed ceremonially as opposed to abusively—and what we might characterize today as *abusive* versus *healing*, but I didn't have a particular place I'd landed with that inquiry—yet something else to lament as I downed the rest of the drink.

My head spun. Feathery bushes rocked over the sides of the trail, and in the California haze, spider nets drifted and glitzed in streamers. I remembered why many Osages had come to California, and why I was one of them—the dreaded, the envied, the mythic California Osage. At the turn of the century, some came here wealthy but mourning loved ones during the Reign of Terror. My great-grandmother, the one who had married white, had been murdered by her husband for her inheritance, after which her mother and daughter came to California. The lost generation bonded my great-great-grandmother and my iko, whom she parented in an old-time way, leaving me without the full modernizing and healing that might have come down in the line had my great-grandmother not married a white man and died early in the 1920s.

Inky black hearts of fuchsia flowers scratched my bare arm. Their petals resembled the pattern of a scarf I had given to a woman holding a small child who asked for it when I last sat at my favorite café in Palo Alto. It was the spot where Julius said all the sluts go. I liked his unorthodox (if basic) manner of speaking, and that was part of my problematic womanhood, which was set up to reinforce men so as to make me a desirable choice for them. Whatever… I liked that café for the culture of the regulars, who carried notebooks and wore headphones, and to whom style mattered, but not in that androcentric, polished way of the profligate faux-moral San Francisco urbane. This place belonged to the anarchists. And if that made them sluts, so be it. This place belonged to the people.

The seagulls cast their shadows as I hiked, and I kept thinking about Café Venetia. One cold evening in particular with the full moon rising. Chianti with caprese cake. And the sense I was wearing the cloak and palimpsest of all of my past selves: aerospace journalist fresh out of college, writing for small Internet blogs and breaking airline technical news that made stocks move; yoga teacher who knew the names of minerals because she had written for *Avionics* and was often forced to refer to such materials in terms of aircraft electronics; teacher studying her language, hoping to help revitalize it but only coaching a few tribal women and friends in the basics of alignment, and mopping the studio so that white women visiting the famous chef in town would not write a ruinous Yelp review; interior designer who got an escape-town job through desperate nepotism; temp who became full-time through many nights of four hours' sleep, and who sat downtown watching groups of confident thirtysomethings in well-fitted jackets order hors d'oeuvres and beer. On that cold night, I had left my spot with a to-go coffee and turned off University to find my great-grandmother's spirit. At first I only sensed her walking beside me, and I did not turn to address her because this seemed rude. The passing cracks in the sidewalk held my gaze as I wondered what she wanted. But of course, they always came to visit because of what *I* wanted. And what I needed to ask, I was afraid to say. My questions: Why did you pass from Black to white? And why did you marry the German who took you away from your home in New Orleans? But it didn't matter, what I asked. Eventually, she would answer the questions. So I started gently: "How do you feel?"

"I'm angry!"

I held my coffee steadily and slowed as two mothers in yoga pants crossed our path. My grandmother often said that she was angry. "Why?" I prodded.

"Because my husband lied. He took me from my family for a poorer life than I'd had in New Orleans! He had a family bakery, I thought he was a safe choice."

"So you married him to be safe?"

"Yes."

I, too, had chosen men because of the impression of safety they gave. "Is that why your mother married your father? To be safe?"

"My mother was from South Dakota. She was a child of rape by a Frenchman. She had no status among her own, and she was terrorized by fear. My father was also Native by his mother, a mixed freedwoman who had a French lover. So those two fled the French in one another, and they were happy. I married the son of a man named Reuben Israel. Is there any wonder why he came from Germany to this land, and why he felt safer with a mixed woman?"

I pictured her family, all of them mixed, my great-great-grandparents painting houses, hiding within a ritualistic Catholicism in which they found comfort.

"But we were so poor. And we lived on the colored side of town. Though both of my parents were colored, the Frenchman showed in my skin and face, so I never had a choice to make, I was taken as mixed in my neighborhood, and as white outside of it. Joe, with his blue eyes and blond hair, fell in love with me. And the French hated the Germans. I thought, why not? He was a recent immigrant, and lived in Baltimore with his family bakery."

She told me, also, that her grandmother was a traditional woman of a tribe she had refused to name, or else had forgotten along with her language. She said her father's mother was "immoral," and that both of her grandfathers were men on whose graves she would have spat.

"But I loved my husband," she kept saying. "He made me laugh."

"Did you die of anger, in the end?" I asked, but she ignored the question and so I thanked her for sewing my grandmother's communion dress and making her and her siblings birthday cakes, two details my grandmother had always remembered. I was crying. There was nothing to say in the cold, with the tears on my face, my affect sad, hers angry, my face shining in the stars, hers invisible. We passed a crossroads, and I waited until the quieter neighborhoods to speak again.

"What did you think of my grandmother?" I asked her. "She always describes herself as being stupid, and that she couldn't *do* anything. She says, 'I was such a dummy,' but she was always reading books." I stated this to let her know that I had studied my family as best I could.

"She was good, quiet, afraid—useless! The youngest," she repeated, acknowledging the little I knew.

"Why didn't you teach her to cook?"

"She was too young to work, but she wasn't good at school, either, she just feared me until I was out of sight."

I did not ask her about why she thought my grandmother had married my papa, because we both knew that with her fear of bearing the child of a rape, she had run away from home, and upon being returned by her father, she had married the first man who asked. It was no wonder, my own fly-by-night behavior—given the coattails of these fleeing, desperate women.

"What about my mother?" I said.

The old woman shook her head, waved her hand. We both viewed my mother the same way. The last time I'd seen her, we went to a reggae concert at a bar in the Caribbean and she kept flirting with the men. I am standoffish toward unknown men, but she was friendly, chatty, full of enthusiastic attention. Nonetheless, I missed her greatly. I cried as my great-grandmother spoke about the constellations, the shape of family tragedies, the resulting sexual fear and brokenheartedness that never healed, ending in affairs and drinking.

"My mother broke up with my father," I said. "She knew he wasn't a respectable person."

"He was persuasive, good with words, smart and tricky. She hid inside of him."

I sighed, exhausted. My drink was lukewarm. I understood that my mother saw the white men in her family as too colonial and patriarchal, the Black men as facing overwhelming racism, and so had chosen a mixed man, hoping to find middle ground among her generational examples of manhood. She wanted a man who would not view her with racism, but who would also be light-skinned enough to avoid attracting the racism of others. I thought this was problematic and sad.

"And me?" I said.

"You've cleared things away from your life, things that created my silence." The moon moved behind clouds and I put on a walking meditation. It was my favorite, led by a brown woman with a confident and kind voice. Women of color today are different than we used to be. We have more options now and it makes our demeanors harder and our hearts softer. Not so long ago, women had to use tricks to find a safe man, and it is still often true. We were silent and walked until the coffee had gone cold. I wished her a good night and her presence receded.

Her husband had kept the preserved braid of her hair in a trunk after she died, and used it to scare her children. I understood more why she liked Julius, who was both weird and hilarious. I had called him then, to show him the moon in the sky on FaceTime, and I called him again now as I finally landed on the beach, hoping to show him the moon visible over the sea in the afternoon light. He did not pick up. We had last met at the pub whose inner walls were covered in small naval miniatures and featured wax statues of palace guards. We had both ordered variants of the shepherd's pie and he had toasted me, joking in poor taste, "Let's colonize the world!"

I did not return his pretend Englishman toast and waited until bread pudding to tell him I wanted to break up. Before that night, I had started conversations Julius thought were breakups by saying things like: "I am going to go to my cousin's for a week," or "I am not happy with things between us right now, and you not being happy with me; it makes me think we won't last," or "If you ever yell at me like that again, I am not going to be able to deal with that," or "If I had my car back from my brother, I would leave right now." At the pub, he knew it was real.

As I took the folding easel out of my bag, my joints cracked repeatedly. My wrists and ankles protested as I set my paints and palettes out on a blanket. My Love rested on the other side of the blanket because the wind was strong and he knew I needed help holding it down. I mixed first yellow, then cyan, magenta, a black-brown tone, and then more blues in darkening shades. Last, I plopped a dollop of white on my tray and dipped my brush in the darkest blue, then dabbed the canvas as sand blew onto it and stuck in foregrounded strokes outlining two glasses filled with black and tan, a bubble foam topping white and merging with the foam of a wave. I painted two of the beers in honor of the night when I'd drunk both our drinks and ended things. Later that night, after he'd left me with the bill, I had hiked down to this very beach.

My parting words still in the air between us, he'd simply left without a word. Not long after that, a paternal grandmother had told me to take my ex back or get a new man, and I had to tell her the ex wanted San Francisco, he was about his American life, and I was trying to shut that down. All of this is why I was sick of marriage advice from the ancestors on my father's side, so I had turned to a maternal focus with my grandmother and the soup. I thought they might like a painting describing my grief.

Above the cliffs, I studied House RGB on its spot peeking through the rock, the last gift from Julius, at least in that he'd designed it. I'd paid for materials and construction, and chosen the name, after the red of exterior brick, the blue of the ocean through the windows, and the enveloping green of jungalow décor. On the sand, My Love and a seagull began to circle one another gracefully around a bit of driftwood. I performed the three gestures I had devised earlier that morning to recall the tarot cards I had pulled as I made the offering: six of wands (three fingers on each hand pointed out in a gesture of prowess); eight of swords (four fingers on each hand moving out from the mind to open it); three of pentacles (one hand gesturing across the horizon, including all).

I added these gestures to my painting as the surf roared and a granular crust dappled the foam of my first painted beer. I tied the canvas to the easel so the string intersected the painting, serving as the horizon line just above the top of the second beer. Above the horizon in small letters, I wrote, *space*.

The ocean wetted the edge of my blanket. It was time to go home and cook. I gathered my things for the hike, visualizing Julius standing near the house with a chic but somehow mournful new haircut. I climbed without stopping and collapsed at the top with my half-painted canvas, out of breath. The painting's upper half shone unevenly in clear primer spelling the word *Interdependence* in paint. The word struck me as interesting, but I did not remember painting it.

"I am happy," I said, and listened to the wind swirling about me. I felt ready to stand up.

My Love and I hurried into the house as the sky thundered and clouds broke in a heavy rain. I slid on my teal velvet robe with a silk lining, which I had sewn by hand; put on some oatmeal; and went for my pipe, which I loaded and began to smoke. I opened a bottle of Velvet Devil, too, and poured a glass, and then went to build a fire. I thought of the beginning of a story my mother had once told me of my father sitting among dozens of lit candles and smoking a cigar. I could not remember the rest of the story; nor did I really want to think about my father. So I lit a match under the scraps of paper and kindling and watched the flames catch the wood.

Next, I turned on the record player. Lightning danced on the water. Thunder sounded and a sudden draft of air turned me toward the front door. It was open. My Love ran to Julius, barking, but my former lover stood in the foyer like a specter with rain streaming down his back.

His right hand held a bottle of prosecco, and in his left there was a stack of mail.

"Your mother says hello," he said, and handed me the mail with a smile.

I couldn't help but move toward him, and as I did, he traced his fingers along his lapel, where there was fastened a small pin, one he had coveted for a long time, which marked him as one of a select group of recognized environmentally protective architects. Unlicensed designers couldn't join this fellowship, and the gleaming button meant he'd achieved two of his life goals.

"You're an architect," I said, and hugged him. I had missed him, and it felt so good.

"Yes," he said. He pressed his hands into my back, lovingly, so that I panicked with the idea that he would kiss me if I looked at him. I pulled away by placing my hand firmly on his chest and using the gesture to separate us. It was a suggestive way to distance us, and he didn't take offense. Instead, he moved his attention to the furniture and nodded with a slow gasp.

"Wow…It looks *so good* in here."

He eyed my velvet and silk robe and my pipe. I offered the pipe to him as we moved toward the fire.

He puffed. "I guess you started up with the smoking jacket routine when I left, eh?"

"When you left?"

"I was the one who walked away," he said.

Julius sat and smoked and sighed in pleasure while My Love winced with each sigh. My mind was clouded with the banal sense that something was happening. Julius was visible in the mirror, posed like a picture behind me, with my third eye showing in a raised vein. It was 7:37.

A knock on the door.

"Who is that?"

"A spirit?" I said—joking, of course. When I answered, no one was there. "Spirits."

"Yes. I'll take a drink," he said.

"Then you better start making one," I said.

"But don't you miss taking care of me?"

Five minutes later, another knock at the door. This time there was a package, with a delivery person receding. Julius came up behind me and called out.

"Hey!" he said, and the man stopped. "Are you creeping around?"

The man turned back to his truck without answering, but Julius stepped out. "Just do your job!" he yelled.

"Why would he be creeping around in this weather? I told you it was spirits," I scolded, but his easy rowdiness made me smile as he came back inside.

"Wathila^ ashkape," I said, which means *he gets mad easy*. I wanted him to recognize the phrase, but his face was blank with ignorance. That irritated me. The only Osage he had ever learned was "i^kshe mi^kshe," a nonsense phrase he'd made up that didn't translate to anything, except maybe vaguely connoting the idea of something being *inside you*, though ungrammatical.

I exhaled. "Creeping around?" I said, my voice pitching low. "Why would you say that?"

He was surprised that I challenged him. He just stood there, staring me right in the eyes. I had to make an effort to do nothing, to simply breathe. In the past, I would have said nothing in the first place, knowing that challenging his masculine posturing could lead to an escalation. But now it didn't matter. Any loss of temper would only lead to his leaving. So I was testing him, and he knew this. Finally, he turned away with only a shrug.

The package. It was from my Realtor friend, the same who had sent me the tincture. Indeed, she was from a long line of traditional medicinal workers, and her nickname was La Brujita. What would she make of the two knocks at my door? Out the window, there was a steady stream of frigid mist, blown along at a ninety-degree angle that made the trees creak and bend in the howling cold. Julius wandered into the kitchen muttering that he would make tea for a hot toddy and in a burst of speedy wet air, my great-great-grandmother glided through a window pane. I tried waving her away but it was no use. She was an ancestor of the Hill People, whose parents hid their children away rather than have them sent to boarding schools for Natives. This meant she was quite good in a sneak-up, and she deftly crossed the room and sat down behind the couch, out of sight but within earshot.

"Do you know now what you want in a man?" she asked.

I went to my chair nearest the door and fiddled with my earrings, feeling disembodied, like my spirit was over my body rather than inside it. Julius returned with me still hovering there, half a foot above myself, thinking about the difference between our cultural values (mine: responsibility, reciprocity, equity, humility, assertive communication, and kindness; his: high standard of living, healing, groundedness, harmony, exchange). I cut my own thought off and dropped back in, because I could hear him thinking, too; he was worrying about a ring—that I would guess that it was in his pocket, which I did; it was a good reason for him to have come.

He faced me and all the lights went out.

"You can sleep on the couch," I told him. "The storm's too much to drive in."

I slept quick and dreamlessly until the visiting ancestor, named D'Achinga, woke me at dawn and threw arrows in my brain. I went out onto the balcony, wet with rain under an enduring but tired drizzle and reflected on the ways I felt insufficient. How I had needed a man. I had almost risked getting pregnant just to try to get one. And that I had only left each man when I saw that he would not give me the child or the attention that I wanted.

"It is I who put the desire for a child in you," said D'Achinga. "Why don't you go back?"

I knew she meant Oklahoma. I threw my hands up. "You heard him say he wanted me to stay in California, and you told me in that dream to stay with him."

"You only have to keep finding ways to help."

"Pardon me?" I didn't know what she was talking about. "I'm not wanted there," I said.

"Then take the girls you know back and offer one of them. Your tribe is small."

I wanted to scream but I laughed. "Okay," I replied noncommittally.

D'Achinga didn't seem impressed.

I didn't have to look to know she was no longer behind the couch. I pulled myself up and went to the coatrack, where I reached into the pocket of Julius's jacket, pulling out the ring.

"Okay," I said to the ring.

"Babe," Julius said. I turned in shock, but I could not even react properly as being *caught*, because behind him, my father appeared in his usual way, blustering forward without preamble.

"I have been wanting to speak to you for years; I am sure that you regret not speaking to me before my death, but seeing as you have set out gifts for me, I've decided to counsel you."

"No," I said, and backed away. I could barely move.

"What?" said Julius. He looked right and left.

"Get the bitter powder," I told him. "In the kitchen, on the counter by the flour canister."

He ran for it.

"I demand to know why you would not speak to me. What was your criticism of me?"

I told him, my voice shaking, that I had already said everything in the letter I'd burned.

"I know," he said. "I didn't contribute in a genuine way even though I claimed my tribe. I complained of being victimized without taking real responsibility for my own actions. But you're a hypocrite. You don't do those things, either."

It was difficult for me to tolerate his defensive apology, but I refrained from screaming at him. Whenever he spoke, I felt such an overwhelm of rage that I could have kicked a hole in the wall. But the only way I showed any of my irritation was with a slow, tired blink. "Are you done?" I said. This was necessary, as a precaution, because if he perceived that someone had interrupted him he would fly into a rage.

"Yes," he said, with an open, childish satisfaction turning his old face as smug as a pig's.

"I noticed your emphasis of the word 'but'," I said. I dipped my finger in the bag of herbs Julius handed me and put that finger inside my mouth. I closed my eyes and called on the ancestors. I called my mother, who had shunned Catholic rituals but liked medicinal and plant-based work. She failed to appear. Instead, it was one of the grandmothers of my maternal line, Jane, who materialized; she was the one I had offered the soup. As soon as her form took shape, my father receded to a spot behind the couch where his great-grandmother D'Achinga had been. Instead of spitting at him, I took three breaths and waited for the bitter powder to reach all throughout my veins.

I spoke: "I figure that I will have to go another generation before women can get respect. Because the negotiation of respect takes time and if I am another body made as a sacrifice to the gods of patriarchy in order to ultimately neutralize them, what does it matter to me, who came from a long line of women who married, remarried, married, married, remarried, all to find a man who might treat them well? And you." I pointed at him, and he bared his teeth because he believed in the old saying that those who are pointed at will die. "Something goes west," I said.

And like the setting sun, he went back to the spirit world.

My great-grandmother spoke. "Necessity is the mother of invention. Although you have no inventions, you have necessity, and the latter will follow. You should forgive your father for teaching you a poor way of living, because he learned that from the nuns at boarding school."

Outside, I knew my ancestors lingered in the grass, trembling in a misty wind, waiting. I felt tears form in my eyes. I was angry at continuously being asked to be here, among the living, without what I felt was enough support.

"What do you want me to do?" I whispered. My eyes blurred as I walked, and though I wanted to lie down in the grass, I kept going, knowing what they wanted. There was a place about a half mile along the coast, toward a river that fell onto the beach. They wanted me to go there, because we were water people, and they thought that this was what I needed. It was what they wanted, anyway. In the pocket of my teal robe, I felt the herbs still in there. I walked faster and plucked flowers as I went, humming and breathing in the moisture in the air so as to try to think more positive thoughts. My Love came galloping behind me, knowing I was on my way to the waterfall that scared him, but he couldn't let me go alone and knew how I was drawn there. I offered him the flowers in my hand to smell, and he sneezed. The ancestors kept appearing. We kept following.

We neared the forest line and the house disappeared from view.

"We're not far; you can hear it rushing," I told My Love.

I wished that My Love would bark, but he was punitively silent, with not even a huff. He was barely panting. I stopped and confronted him with my gaze. *I only care about you*, I imagined him saying. I was ready for someone to let me off the hook, and maybe I was losing my mind, but this dog was the only person I had, and, I realized, the only one who had been keeping me hopeful and socialized in this place where I felt lonely and desperate. We walked northeast and I remembered the legend of a woman around here who had jumped into the waterfall, wishing to end her life, but had survived only to find something good.

I spoke what I remembered of the story aloud. "In the physics of the fall, and with the exact placements of river rock below, chance allowed the woman to slip into a clear spot where the current rounded her around the largest, smoothest rock. In a long slide, she floated downriver until she washed ashore at a homeless camp. She was scratched up but unbroken, and spent several weeks visiting as she healed, eating stews and such made from ingredients that the people had foraged and listening to their stories. Finally, she recovered, and returned home."

"Hm. Is that a true story?"

I jumped and screamed. It was Julius.

"I thought you wouldn't see us when we were beyond the tree line."

"I had a feeling," he said.

We came to the bridge and I peered over the side where the water rushed beneath. When I turned to look at the waterfall itself, there was D'Achinga and another mother, Chi Mi Hun.

I greeted them by the names of their husbands. "Du Bourbonnais and Vallée."

One from Québec, the other from France. My Love sat his head beneath my hand, Julius now out of earshot, scrambling on rocks and photographing the waterfall. I remembered in Pawhuska, when the women I worked with had called me oblivious.

Chi Mi Hun spoke: "You are right that we are humbled people, daughters of Claremore and Pawhuska who lived beside wild rivers, as well as those men of good families who traveled south in search of fur. Politics compelled us both to wed foreigners, but we were honored."

D'Achinga spoke. "You are no longer wanting to die, because you have learned that people do not want to be against each other, and their work is to find out how to have peace."

"You're the person who protected me all those mornings I woke up for so many years, when I was young, and all I could do was weep."

"Yes. And look, you don't have to be here. But don't you see things are getting better?"

Hearing that I had a choice about whether to be here or not made me feel less pressure. I cried again, but tried to stop myself, not wanting my eyes to be at their puffiest for my proposal. I understood that this relationship might not work out, and that it was also possible that it might. I was okay with both outcomes, and proud of myself for acknowledging living was what I needed then. The flowers were resting on the arms of the bridge. I smelled the fragrant blooms and offered them to my ancestors, but they moved back into the water. I dropped the bouquet down over the ledge as Julius returned and put his arms around me there, still with my right hand on My Love, and we all watched the bundle slip between the rocks and away, into the ocean.

THE GOOD MEDICINE OF THE LIGHT

In the old days, when the Little Ones lived around the three rivers which braided into one, there was a Tsizho medicine woman named The Light who was honorably married to a Hunka warrior named Standing Bear. When her husband was not fighting the enemies of the Little Ones or hunting buffalo, The Light went with him to skip stones in the water and float on their backs. During the cold months, they wrapped themselves in furs and watched the sunrise in the gray-blue fog of the prairie. Their love was like a mist under Grandmother Moon dancing on snow. But before they had even received the gift of a child, Standing Bear died in battle. The Light was studying for the spider tattoo with her teacher when Standing Bear's brother The Rain brought the news.

The Rain rode into camp carrying a red flag that the Little Ones had retrieved from their enemies, and he told how Standing Bear had given his life in battle to save The Rain's own life. The women began keening and The Light stood at the door of her teacher's lodge and felt the ka^ slip right out of her body into the earth. Ka^ is that which comes from Waka^da, the sacred force behind the growth of plants and the flow of blood, that which gives life, as The Light had hoped to give life to a child, and also that which takes life, as Standing Bear's life had died.

The Light fell to the ground. "Ozhu mi^kshe," she said, because she was like a vessel without any water. Meaning, *I am empty.* Years before, The Light's father had also died in battle. It was difficult for The Light to move or speak, and as the moons passed after her husband's death, The Light's body felt heavier to her, such that it was difficult for her to speak or move. A shadow fell over her thoughts, and the Little Ones took note of her pitiful condition with kindness, all except for her mother's second husband, a man called Uncle.

If the Little Ones brought The Light persimmons and pecans, saying, "Da^he ni^kshe tsi wihko^bra," *I want you to be all right,* Uncle saw the gifts piled beside the fire of The Light and said, "Dada^ shdatse na^pe? Ka^ze a^nakoe omizhe akaha ala. Othushima schi^a^. Tsele wida xo wie. Da ono^bre shkaxe wiko^bra. Owe, ka^ze, hko^brai^ke! Pa!" which means, *What do you call this? Put the fruit on top of the mat, you are in the way and my stomach is growling. I want you to make nicely cooked meats for me. I do not want that raw fruit! Buh!*

The old man went on, saying The Light needed a distraction, and to focus on other people. She had already been keening at dawn, and that was enough crying. She had better be useful to him, as he, too, had lost a son in the death of Standing Bear and grief made him hungry.

The Light cried as she began to cook.

"Ma^thi!" he said. *Hurry up!*

At this, she burst into tears, which made Uncle even angrier. "Thali nie hko^bra. Thi^datse i^ke ma^zhi. Wakats'a zhi^?" *I want you to be well. You are not fatherless. Do you think everything is about you?*

When The Light's mother heard this, she did nothing. She was too bereft from the loss of her first husband, and it was all she could do to go on. Although she knew her daughter should remarry, she wanted to have her help to cook and meet all the demands of Uncle, who demanded to be treated with special respect, as if he were one of the wise counselors called Little Old Men.

The only way The Light could get a rest from Uncle was in her studies for the spider tattoo, and in visiting her grandmother.

"Witsoshpa!" the old woman would say when she saw her granddaughter.

"Iko!" said The Light. And the two of them would sew moccasins, and The Light would rest and take a nap by the fire while old withered hands clutched tanned buckskin.

One day, about a year after Standing Bear's death, the grandmother heard that one of the Little Old Men, the youngest of them, who was about forty years of age, had asked Uncle and his wife for The Light's hand in marriage. But Uncle was too selfish and turned him down. This made the grandmother very angry, and she resolved to intervene. When The Light came to visit her, she told her to go out into the tall grass, and walk down the hills until the meat of her legs shook and she felt wonderful in the arrowgrass and coyote mint.

"Mi ishdakie," she said. *Bless yourself with the sun.*

The grandmother had sent a message to the Little Old Man who was in love with The Light, telling him to go out and meet her in the tall grass. The Little Old Man had agreed, even though a bush love marriage was not honorable, because he was so in love with The Light. And while the grandmother hated to see her granddaughter without any status, it was better for her to have a bush love marriage with the Little Old Man than to languish in Uncle's lodge until she was so old she could not even bear any children.

The Light did not know the half of her grandmother's plan, but she loved to walk.

"Etsida bre dv mi^kshe," she said. *I'm going now*, and she left.

Past her plot of purple corn, down the hill of red grasses, soon she came to the tall grass. As she walked, rays of sun danced through moving clouds so that warmth fell on the earth in traveling spots. The Light ran as fast as she could to stay with the warmth of the sun, until she came to the edge of the woodlands. There she prayed.

"Waka^da, zhaninazhi eihe. Howaikishki bre env owani zhi eihe. Ozhu mi^kshe. Tsidwi Waka^daki i^kshe pshie azhi ozhu mi^kshe a^kadxai. Kaci shi eko^ datsi^ epe. Hai tsi azhihe bruts'aki. A^pizhi. Na^tse eko^i^ke. Dada^ pizhi awanazhi. Akilaibri. Kopshe."

Great Mystery, she said, *I'm restless. Any place I go, I feel afraid. I'm empty inside. Tomorrow it will be that way again. I'm not doing well. My heart is a living wound. Something bad is standing on me. That's how I am. That is all I can say.*

As The Light talked, the wind moved her hair about, and she heard something behind her.

It was a rattlesnake, and The Light backed into the brush as he spoke. "Da^he ni^kshe tsi wihko^bra," said the snake. *I want you to be all right.* He shook his tail at her, and warned that she would wring her own heart out if she stayed in Uncle's grasp.

The Light was afraid of the snake and his words, so she turned and ran until she came to a creek where a doe drank water at the bank. She stopped short and the doe raised its snout to her.

"Da^he ni^kshe tsi wihko^bra," said the doe, and as the animal spoke, a crayfish wriggled in the stream, rubbing its shell in the four colors of the mud of those waters.

"Da^he ni^kshe tsi wihko^bra," said the crayfish.

It was noon, and The Light washed her face in the water like the doe and prayed to the four directions. Then the doe ran south, and The Light followed, picking little yellow flowers as she went, ones her grandmother had shown her, and chewing them like gum.

The creek flowed into a stream, and soon The Light came to the place where the water leaked into a river, and that river then met with two others in the place called the Middle Waters.

There, in the braided waters, she saw a person with waves rippling at his belly. He whispered, and the trees bent down low over the surface to hear what he was saying. The Light climbed into the reeds and the person turned to her.

"I am Wazhazhe," said the person. "Make yourself of me and purify all that comes to you. Soon you will go to a new place, and you will see new flowers grow in the rain. Then Grandfather Sun will paint your forehead in rainbows. Make a song of purifying, and then go."

With this, Wazhazhe fell into the water. The Light saw that water was the substance Wazhazhe embodied. She thanked the water.

"Wewinai," she said. *Thank you for this.*

With this, The Light made her way back to the tall grass, but Spider stopped her on the way. Unlike the other animal people, Spider did not address The Light. She waited. The Light wanted to be careful with her words, because she was studying to have the stylized spider symbol tattoo, and it was said that the spider took her home with her wherever she went, and that she had only to wait for all things to come to her and therein break their necks. She could not think of the right thing to say, so she said nothing, and learned without words that Spider wanted to tell her of patience.

As the sun set, the Little Old Man left the tall grass. It was then that Spider moved and let The Light pass. It was dark now.

"Mi^o^pa," The Light called to the moon, but its light was behind the clouds. The laying-down grass in the meadow began to move with a great wind, and a melody entered The Light's ear. She sang to herself her song and hurried to tell the Little Old Men a song, but before long, she hurt her foot in a buffalo rut, and though she cried out, no one heard her. To comfort herself, she sang her song. The melody is mysterious, and the words tell of how grass moves in the wind.

While The Light sang her song, far away in the camp Uncle was also singing. His song told a story of himself as a person named Gray Fox, a misshapen and lonely animal with a friend called Little Turtle, whom he depended on as his special helper. Gray Fox told Little Turtle everything, but Gray Fox worried someone would say he was tricking Little Turtle by always talking to her in tricking patterns, making her feel guilty to keep her there so she would give him everything he wanted, and claiming that this was right and best for Little Turtle although this was just a trick he was playing on her and everyone and, most of all, himself. Uncle's song claimed that Little Turtle was lucky that someone would deem her worth the effort it took to trick someone like that, and always think of them.

Uncle wanted desperately to share his song, but The Light would not come home.

He raged into the grandmother's lodge. "Howaiki the?" he asked. *Where is she?*

"Atsi apaithe," said the grandmother. *She's camping.*

"Ha^koda?" said Uncle. *Why? What is going on?*

The old woman thought of the Little Old Man and smiled.

"Dada^?" said Uncle, his eyes wet with anger. *What is this?*

"Dowa akahida akilaithi thiape," she said. *Well, somebody is a man on the fringes, eh?* Then she said, "Ono^bre akacpa. Li^ka etsi wano^bre." *The food's covered. Sit and eat.*

But the old man was so angry he left without saying another word.

"Dada^ pizhi ekiothi^ka!" she cried out after him. *Don't you do something bad!*

Uncle went to the lodge of The Rain and told him that The Light was missing. The Rain was friends with the Little Old

Man who loved The Light, and he held his tongue tight, thinking that they were out together in the bush. To everything Uncle said, The Rain replied, "Eko^," in vague agreement.

But as soon as Uncle left, The Rain went to his friend's house.

"Howaiki the?" said the Little Old Man. *Where is she?*

"Ipaho^ mazhi^," said The Rain.

They sat very quietly for a time, and when the night was very late, they got up and rode out on horses, but Uncle was sitting at the door of his tent and he stopped them.

"Howaiki sche?" *Where are you going?*

"Hithi e otse ma^thi^ pshie." *Going out there to search.*

"Tsi tsi hithi." *Come by my house.*

The Little Old Man and The Light went out and the light of the moon cleared as they traveled down the hill on their horses. The Rain thought of The Light like a sister and when he heard her grass song, he felt in his heart that something was wrong.

The Little Old Man's ears were not as good, and he did not hear the song, so The Rain told him to search the other way, and they parted. The Rain came to The Light and saw her singing in the buffalo rut. He didn't want to scare her, so he waited for her to stop crying, faint with hunger and lying in the buffalo rut. He had to wait for a long time before she saw him.

"Pa!" she said finally.

"Kquio," he said. *Come here*. And he lifted her onto his horse and without another thought, he rode and took her to the village on the other side of the woodlands, where he knew they were in need of a medicine woman.

The Light did not ask where they were going, because she was used to Uncle, who said she should be content whatever he did, and who said he never had to do a thing. She was used to being badly treated, and she went along with things because she was used to having no say.

They went into the woodland, crossed the creek, and went up hills, weaving through clusters of rock and trees weeping sap until at last they arrived in the camp at dawn. The Light dismounted, and grasshoppers jumped around her feet like shooting stars. There were two births going on in the village, and the people needed dried moss and cherry bark. They said as a medicine woman, she could have her own lodge. The Light remembered her own home, and she was ashamed that she had let Uncle make her so weak.

She thanked The Rain.

"Wa^tho thida ana^k'o. Na^tse ma^thi^ tsi wihko^bra," he said. *I heard your song. I want you to have a calm and normal heart.*

The Light knew that her grandmother and Waka^da and the animals and Wazhazhe and The Rain had all helped her and that now she would have to take back her ka^.

A medicine man gestured for her to help him with the births, and took her leave.

To The Rain, she said, "Kashikada^ iwithe hdv^ mi^kshe. Ina^pa." *I will see you again. Be careful.*

"Eko^," said The Rain, and he rode away.

The medicine man turned into the woodland and The Light followed him. He had a serious mouth, thin legs, and his chest was small and puffed out. He did not look at anything directly, and his hair was not in a scalp lock but moved on his shoulders. When he turned to point out the cherry tree, she saw the tattoos on his arms.

She leaned over to pick up some dried moss and looked him in the face to see if he was afraid of her. He was not. She let her buffalo robes hang around her shoulders.

"Kikiazhi," she said. *Butterfly, it flies weird.* This was her nickname for him, because she thought he was odd but beautiful.

"I^shda Ni," he said. *Watery Eyes.*

Then, without a word, they kissed, and stared at one another for a moment before they returned to camp with the cherry bark and moss. As they walked, she touched his fingers covered in zigzag tattoos, and he told her that his first wife had died and it was time for him to have sons.

"Pahithe," he said. *Come to my house.* And he said that he knew her husband was dead.

"Eko^," she agreed, and she was not sad to find herself in this new bush love marriage.

The birth went well, and when they came out of the lodge, it was night and a child came and whispered in the medicine man's ear. Then the child ran and the medicine man scolded her.

"Nika akihe apai, shena." *There's a man hanging around, waiting.*

"A^hakie," she said. *I don't quite understand.*

"Ha^koda?" he said. *What is going on?*

She told him that she was not betrothed, and that the old man who would come after her was her uncle, and that he was very strange and she had to get away from him.

The medicine man turned away from her and went in the direction the child had gone. The Light was afraid, but she followed him, too, and when they came to the middle of the camp, there was the Little Old Man.

He had been a warrior in his time, and he was named for the colors of the sunset hue. Ze Zhutse Eko^, *Like yellow and red.*

Some children were around a fire, and The Light sat with them and began to help them separate dried cedar from the branch. Meanwhile, the men spoke and The Light prayed that whatever happened, she would meet with ka^.

The men talked until the fire was low, and then the Little Old Man left. The Light heard the crunch of the medicine man's moccasins on the pebbles around the fire and she dared to look up from her cedar. He placed a rock on the fire and sat beside her.

The Light put her work down and the children and she and the medicine man all watched the rock redden until, after a time, it burst. The Light saw the power behind this action and understood that was a power driving the Little Old Man.

Finally, the medicine man told her that the Little Old Man wanted her as a Sits Beside Wife, or a second wife to keep him company.

"Wawibrilai," he said. *So make up your mind.*

The Light knew that to be a Sits Beside Wife was honorable, and to be a bush love wife was not. With no one to give her away here, and no horses to gift, she could not have any status. But back in her old camp, she was reminded of Standing Bear and also she saw that her Uncle had all but made her into his Sits Beside wife anyway. She did not want that any longer.

"She mi^kshe," she said. *I'm sitting here.*

The medicine man nodded. "Na^tse wida okupa akxai." *My heart is filling over.*

Ze Zhutse Eko^ the Little Old Man had heard this. He stepped back and cast a long shadow in his otter cap and heavy robes. He drew his knife.

"Nika zhi," he said. *You little man.*

The medicine man stood and took a knife hanging from his waistband.

"Ekiothi^ka!" said The Light. *Don't do that!* And then, her ka^ really came back, right up from the earth into her toes and throughout her whole body via her veins. She picked up the bits of warm rock and she held them out in her palm.

"E akido^pa. Akilaibri," she said. *You're looking at me, this rock, that's how I am.*

They understood that she was a broken woman, and that it was her choice.

So Ze Zhutse Eko^ and The Light touched hands. Something strong passed between them. Then the Little Old Man turned, climbed on his horse, and left without a word.

The Light wiped away her tears and touched the medicine man's curly hair. "Ma^pshewai, wewinai," she said. *Ancestors, all you up to something, thank you.*

The chinquapins shook their leaves on the edge of the wood, and the medicine man brought her cherries, dried meat, and persimmon cakes. They went into his lodge and they ate.

When Uncle heard of The Light and how she had regained her ka^ in the new place with a bush love husband, he called her a dirty witch. But the people of her old camp said that her medicine must be very strong, to regain her ka^ like that. The Rain taught them her song, and when warriors died, the people sang it to their widows. Waka^da would finally bless The Light with children, they said. And so it was that The Light used her medicine to heal her living wound.

ACKNOWLEDGEMENTS
𐓂́𐓆𐓂𐓈𐓄𐒰́ 𐓍𐓂𐒰 𐒽𐓂͘𐒴𐒰

Wihso^ka, wihta^ke, thachi piche wewinai, zani wawihoipi. Pa^ha^le ithae shko^shda che wewinai. Ie toe ekipshe hko^bra atx-a^he. Ithak'utse hda mikshe. I^thak'utse hda a^katxai. Wahko^ta wato^pa pita^ thak'ewathapi hko^bra.

Brothers and sisters, I'm grateful for your being here, and I wish to address you all with respect. First, I want to say that I am grateful that you wanted me to speak. I want to say a few words. I will try my best. As the Great Spirit looks down on us, I want us to be blessed.

I wrote this book on Wazhazhe, Cherokee, Tongva, Tewa, Ohlone, Comanche, Kiowa, Cheyenne, and Ute land with support from the Osage Nation Foundation, the Mid-America Arts Alliance, the Native Arts & Cultures Foundation, and a PEN America Writers' Emergency Fund. Thank you to my cousin Aimee, Auntie Mary, my friend DezBaa, and Darwin (whom I dearly love) for providing me with food and space, in addition to the folks at Elsewhere Studios and Northwestern Oklahoma State University. I thank my mentors for encouraging me, particularly Toni Jensen and Brandon Hobson. I am also here because of my parents, Brian and Holly Hicks.

I have had many teachers, and the first was Sydney Blair at the University of Virginia, may she rest in peace. At UC Davis and the Institute of American Indian Arts, many taught me about writing and the writing life, and I'm deeply grateful. Among those who influenced my writing are Lucy

Corin, Yiyun Li, Terese Marie Mailhot, and Pam Houston, in addition to Toni and Brandon. I also thank my friends Carla and Shaina, as well as my language friends, Bill Hamm and Ruby Hansen Murray. *McSweeney's* and *Yellow Medicine Review* published earlier versions of "A Fresh Start" and "Brother," and in so doing gave me energy to continue writing. My editor, Chris Heiser of Unnamed Press, was revelatory, transformative, and fun. I'm very grateful to my agent, Jin Auh, who makes me feel understood and found this book a good home at Unnamed Press. I am grateful to Jaya Nicely for depicting Wazhazhe ie orthography in print.

The Wazhazhe ie pictured on the cover of this book means *a calm and normal heart; a content heart*; or *heart stays.* Our hearts as Native people stay with our land and the graves of our ancestors. As I^shdaxi^ have written in publications like *Killers of the Flower Moon* by David Grann, and the associated film by Martin Scorsese, Wazhazhe people endured the Reign of Terror in the 1920s. Some fled to California, where they formed community groups called United Osages of Southern California and Northern California Osage. I thank Wazhazhe people for working to exist in community, gathering where they are. Without these diaspora groups, I would not have come to write this book. As Wazhazhe people become more well-known, I have felt urgency to write this book, so that our own voices will be among those telling our stories.

This book seeks to represent contemporary Indigenous people broadly, but it does not capture the diversity of Indigenous people. Ongoing underrepresentation exists for Black Indigenous persons, and I have not felt able to ameliorate this misrepresentation by myself, though I recommend reading the exquisite work of mixed-Indigenous and African diaspora authors such as Jesmyn Ward, Jamie Figueroa and Honorée Fanonne Jeffers. Some of my ancestors are Creole from New Orleans, in my matrilineal line. Because I come from these people, I feel it is my responsibility to explicitly promote voices of Black and African diaspora Indigenous people. I offer my respect, my listening ear, and my acknowledging eyes.

To the Indigenous people who left their home communities at the time of the Indian Relocation Act of 1956, as well as those who left their communities after attending boarding schools, I offer my thanks for your survivance. To those who felt they had no option but to assimilate, and sold their land as they fell on hard times, I thank you for staying here and doing your best. For disconnected Indigenous people, as well as for people of any culture that is undergoing stress, speaking heritage language presents a restorative experience. I am indebted to disconnected people everywhere who are reconnecting. "Coming home" inspires me to write.

Rematriation is another name for coming home, and the practice broadly holds that ancestral and hereditary cultural reconnection promotes strong mental health and community. My friend, and the writer and therapist Lyrica Fils-Aimé first taught me of this term, and learning about this frame of thought helped me envision new ideas for the book. Rematriation does not hold that peoples must relocate to their original homelands, but I hope that Indigenous nations will become sovereign governors of their own homelands. I am thankful to Indigenous governments for their work to secure tribal recognition for peoples who (unjustly) do not already have federal tribal status, despite making treaties and losing access to their lands due to settler violence.

Tribal nations have sometimes been formed in militaristic, colonial models subordinated to the federal government, but Indigenous scholars and allies are studying ways to reincorporate traditional tribal relationality into tribal governing structures. I thank Indigenous scholars for helping me understand ways to continue forward as a Wazhazhe woman, and

I acknowledge the poetics of Canadian settler Shane Rhodes, who emphasizes that treaties are for settlers, too. The work of Dr. Kim TallBear on polyamory and Native American DNA was also critical to these stories. The writings of N. Scott Momaday taught me what land- and cultural-connectedness mean through story, which is my deepest learning style. Studying with Inés Hernández-Ávila at UC Davis helped me understand the need to cultivate a process of unlearning colonial beliefs to become a good contributor. The process of *un*learning led me to ancestral language as a mode of reconnection, and I thank Mogri Lookout and Chris Cote as well as Cameron Pratt and Stephanie Rapp for guiding me as I have studied and continue to study Wazhazhe ie.

I thank Wazhazhe culture-bearers for working to keep our ways alive as well as making it possible for me to engage our language in this book. I use the word *Wazhazhe* for my people, and *Wazhazhe ie* for our language, but we are also called by the French bastardization *Osage.* Our Nation of living people are also called the Niuko^cka, or Children of the Middle Waters, referring to the rivers that make confluence on our ancestral homelands.

I thank our ancestors, in the visible and invisible worlds, our ancestral homelands, and our waters. Land- and ancestral-based practice will teach us to protect the lands from which we first emerged.